Praise for Ray Else's writing:

" ... some of your writing is beautiful. It is superb. You have tremendous talent."

— Sam Jordison, Galley Beggar Press

"Else obviously has a vivid imagination and some of the story-telling passages are wonderful."

— Allen H. Peacock, Simon & Schuster

"his prose is evocative and he brings fresh sharp insight to family scenes"

— Deborah Futter, Bantam Doubleday Dell

"On Sunday February 23rd I suffered from insomnia and turned on the World Service in the middle of the night. I was absolutely captivated by what I heard. It was your short story 'Surviving on Mexican Shade'."

— John R. Murray, John Murray Publishers

Galley Beggar Press published Ray Else's story *First Kiss* as one of their monthly shorts. This story inspired the First Kiss Mystery novels of which *All that we touch* is the third volume.

Ray Else's short story *Surviving on Mexican Shade* was broadcast by the BBC World Service and included in the Transcontinental Review published by the Sorbonne in Paris. His unfinished work *My Father's Lies*, which includes both *First Kiss* and *Surviving on Mexican Shade*, was shortlisted for a Shakespeare & Company Novella Prize.

Cover Photo by Veronica Else

Ray Else

All that we touch

Ray Else

A Novel: that is, a work of fiction.

DEDICATION

Dedicated to my dear sister Cyndy, who taught me to be mindful of others.

ALL THAT WE TOUCH

She wondered how the world could frown so, and hide from her the truth like a spoiled child keeping his toy to himself.

Volume Three of the First Kiss Mystery Series

Prologue

She was once told that before His All existed there was only God the non-Creator. Like a writer before his first story, He struggled to understand what He was capable of, He hesitated to set His All in motion, for who would appreciate His work?

Who would say, Yes, I love His All, and in so saying, return the Love he put in His work? In His All?

Who would receive His inspiration, His whispers and His confessions, His caresses and His fire?

There was no one.

He despaired, revised His All, created order where once His All was chaos. Added meaning and mystery, added minor gods like beauty, whimsy and desire, added men and women.

Who in their way, sometimes vaguely understood. Who set rules themselves, played gods themselves. Sometimes prayed to God, asking for favors. And sometimes they told him they loved His All. Which moved Him little. For what meaning did that have? They were just His creations, after all.

No, she was once told, God does not desire the love of his creations. God searches for the Love of another Creator. To share His All with Theirs.

Ray Else

1 They're coming for her

"Why me?" said thirty year old Fernanda as she stepped into the shower. "*No entiendo.*"

Why did the FBI suspect her of being a killer? Why did they post men to watch the cabin here in Arkansas? Why did they follow wherever she went?

And what about the others, the holy man in India, the shaman in Peru, why had they declared that she was born to be sacrificed? Not for her own good, but for the good of humankind. She had to die, they said, so the world could keep on spinning.

"*No entiendo!*"

How did she get caught up in this? How could she get out?

She soaped her front. Her breasts felt good, free from their tight wrap. She bent and scrubbed her legs with the *estropajo*. She remembered the bathers they'd seen in the Ganges, in India, waist deep in the green current, sudsing their brown skin. India, the place

1

where her dreams darkened. The place where the madness began.

How did she get caught up in this? How could she escape?

And her dreams, at night, darker still. Worse than India. Mysterious forces sniffed her out, in her nightmares, drew round her like hounds to a feast. Ancient headless bodies, and bodiless heads. She knew what they wanted, though they did not speak in any language she understood. They wished to split open her heart like a pomegranate, to spill the red seeds of her love to sow the entire world.

She did not know how she knew this, but she did.

"They want my love," she told herself, wrapping her arms around her slippery self. Love reserved for her husband Randy, who she loved more than there were sounds in a lifetime. Love reserved for her baby daughter, who she loved more than there was breath in every living being. Take my love and you will destroy all things, she told the horrid figures, when they appeared to her, when she remembered to speak to them. To curse them. To chase them away.

She slowly turned, careful not to slip, as she rinsed away the soap film.

She thought of her husband, Randy. Had it been two years already? Since they married? Poor Randy, himself entangled, labeled by chance, because of the India project, as IBM's 007. All dear Randy wanted to do was program computers for IBM's customers, exercise his expertise - but since India, and then Peru, the only requests to IBM for Randy's services were for everything *but* his programming expertise. From people who wanted him to root out fraud, to get to the bottom of foul play, to solve a murder. Was Fernanda to blame? Perhaps. To some degree. Probably. For Fernanda herself had become newsworthy, for all the wrong reasons.

She should never have agreed to do the interview with PEOPLE Magazine, when they returned from Peru. But she had liked the idea of earning her keep, with what they paid. Until she could finish her training in natural healing and divination. And get the blessing of her shaman teacher, Paro, who she'd met in Peru, his blessing to do divinations by herself.

Most everyone would pay for a divination, to help with a critical decision in their life. Should they, or shouldn't they, marry him or her? Buy that new house? Invest in that new business? Are they are on the right path? Is the one they love faithful? How can they get back the precious love they've lost? People would gladly pay for her help, as a shaman, in addressing these life decisions. And she would love to help. But she wasn't yet ready.

Paro, her teacher, had refused to divine Fernanda's future a second time. After the disastrous divination in the Andes. And she understood. Once was enough. Fernanda, full of love, a faithful wife and now a loving mother, Fernanda was born to be sacrificed. Whatever that meant.

She squirted Argan shampoo onto her palm, replaced the bottle on the shelf, rubbed her hands together and massaged the goo into her full black hair. Worked her fingers through the long strands, let that be a kind of therapy. She turned to face the onslaught of water. Suds swirled on her front, rippled over her stretch marks, plumed down her legs. She felt her worries drain away with the suds. Tranquility, of a sort. Then the cry of the baby. Her baby. She smiled. Nothing lasts forever.

2 PEOPLE

Fernanda made the PEOPLE Magazine cover, not because hers was the cover story but because of the way her lovely face beckoned. The editors knew that her kind of natural Mexican beauty, with its almond eyes, firm red lips, full cheeks embraced by silky black hair …, they knew Fernanda's face would sell a million more copies than a cover picture of a haggard, disgraced cleric. So they put Fernanda, whose story was only three pages long, on the cover, with a small inset of the priest whose story went on for ten.

"She was a human sacrifice" read the caption on page twenty-four, "by Miam S." Here is the entire PEOPLE article, minus the picture of an eight month pregnant Fernanda with Fernanda's IBM sweatshirt-clad husband Randy peeking out from his study:

It's been barely six months since twenty-nine year old Fernanda Guadelupe de Cortez (her maiden name), a Mexican immigrant, a wife and soon to be mother, staggered off a snowy mountain top in Peru. She barely escaped being sacrificed to the gods by members of the Wari tribe, predecessors of the Incas - those who still believe in the ancient ways of placating the gods. She was born to be sacrificed, their shaman told the tribe, and they took him at his word.

"I never thought I would get off that peak," she tells PEOPLE. "I've been cold every day since." She shivers, pulls the handmade Peruvian shawl tighter around her. A monstrous scraping sound shakes the windows, vibrates through the wooden floor, the sound of metal clawing at rock. She glances outside the picture window of their cabin in the Arkansas woods. "Chance, our business partner, is working the mine," she says. "The quartz crystal mine. The mountains around Hot Springs are full of crystal."

Their trip to Peru months ago had started normally enough. Her husband Randy invited her to accompany him on a project for IBM. But shortly after arriving they discovered the real reason Randy had been requested by the Cuzco bank manager was that his son had been kidnapped. He hadn't hired Randy from IBM to work on his computer system. Instead he had hired him with the hope that Randy could get his young son back.

Randy balked. He had no real detective skills. But it seemed the word of his success in India, of his foiling of a kidnapping, had spread. Spread as far as Peru, to this bank manager in Cuzco, who needed help. Fernanda convinced Randy to try to find the man's boy. So try they did. Next thing they knew they were hiking the rugged, steep Inca Trail, complete with Wari porters and a Wari shaman. Then came the fateful divination by the shaman, high in the Andes, where he declared that Fernanda was so full of love that the world could barely hold her. He declared she would be the most perfect human sacrifice, the best in two thousand years. Shortly thereafter Fernanda was whisked away by the porters. Drugged. Placed on the same mountain top where the Wari sacrificed children for a thousand years, buried in the snow to be claimed by the gods. A human sacrifice to Inti and Mama Killa. And to all the mountain spirits.

"I never thought I would get off that mountain," Fernanda repeats, standing up. Her belly extends naturally, in harmony with the rest of her curvy body. She smiles, briefly. Shakes her head.

PEOPLE asks if the lost boy was ever found.

"Randy, my husband," here she motions to the study behind her, "he asked me not to talk about that." She stretches. The shawl nearly falls off her smooth shoulders. "He doesn't really like that I am giving this interview. Too many strange things have been happening, since our honeymoon in India, since our trip to Peru."

She strolls to the picture window.

"Strange things happen even now. *Mira*. Look." She points to the adjoining hilltop, where two men stand in the brush. One has binoculars. "FBI agents. After India, because of what happened there, the murders, the maiming, after what happened, the FBI watch me." She paused then, tried to smile but failed. "They interviewed me, once. Called me Fernanda the Ripper. Accused me of horrible things."

She does not want to talk more about what happened in India.

She opens the front door, pushes wide the screen, moves out onto the porch. An old couple, having paid ten dollars each for the privilege, dig in freshly dumped dirt piles, tailings from the mine. They are searching for loose crystals. They look up for a moment, at the sound of the screen door slamming, then return, as if hypnotized, to their digging.

Honey bees and bumble bees fly about. The air smells of pine and upturned earth. The monstrous strain of machine on stone sounds again, disturbing the flight of the bees.

Fernanda talks about her father, who always claimed she fell to him as a baby from the sky. She never knew her mother. She tells how her father headed up a mariachi band in Mexico. How he taught her to play the trumpet before she could even walk. She toured with the band all over Mexico.

"On tour with my father's band, when I was seven, we visited the ruins of Chichen Itza. And I got lost. Three Mayan men, Indians you know, appeared out of nowhere, dressed the old way, and gave me presents. Before my father found me."

She looks at her palms, as if examining those presents of long ago.

"Flowers," she says. "Herbs? And a gold peso coin."

She suffers nightmares. Ever since India. Worse since the incident in Peru. In a recurring dream a hateful girl tries to convince her that she must die because she has too much love in her.

She excuses herself, steps inside, just as her business partner, Chance, comes up from the mine in dusty overalls. He mounts the porch steps. He is a powerful man, sunburned, handsome despite the scar on his face.

"A big cluster I was prying loose one morning released before I was ready," he says, touching the scar.

He says the FBI are crazy to be following Fernanda. That she is innocent. "I've known her since I graduated high school," he says. "Me and Randy slipped her over the border from Mexico in the trunk of my car. Did she tell you that?"

He wipes his forehead. Looks out at the couple digging in the tailings. He spits.

"Yeah, me and Randy were best pals in high school, back in Texas. We drove to Mexico in my car to celebrate graduation." He pauses to lick his dry lips. "Randy met Fernanda there, the first night. He liked her so much that he made a deal that if she gave him a kiss he'd help her cross the border. Can you believe that? Risk prison for a kiss? And I helped them. But we were all crazy back then."

He knocks a bee from his sleeve. "We were together, a while. Me and her. Years actually. She helped me start the mine. Then Randy returned from Paris." He pauses, glances towards the screen door. "They're married now." He turns his head, looks towards the mounds of tailings. Here and there tiny sparks flare from the dirt, as the perfectly flat faces of half-buried crystals catch the sun. "I'm married too. Have a son. We live over there." He points to a roof just visible on the other side of the mine. He starts down the porch steps.

"I used to call her Freddy," he says, pausing, "though I knew she never liked it."

PEOPLE contacted the FBI to see why they were following Fernanda, and they said to talk to INTERPOL. The authorities at INTERPOL, when questioned whether there was a file on Fernanda the Ripper, or, for that matter, Fernanda the innocent, they refused to give any statement.

Please leave your comments about this article on the new PEOPLE blog at ...

3 *Migas*

"Is she working out OK?" asked Randy from his place at the head of the table. "The nanny, I mean. Constance."

"*Si*," said Fernanda, serving Randy his favorite breakfast of *migas*, eggs fried and scrambled with pieces of corn tortilla. The baby could be heard in the next room; she wasn't exactly crying, but they both could tell that she wasn't happy, either. "Constance is trying to get her to drink my milk from a bottle. To wean her from my breasts. But little Rocky doesn't like the texture of the rubber nipple I think."

"So we can take this trip? Two weeks in Paris? Our second honeymoon? Without the baby?"

Fernanda frowned.

"That was our reasoning, no?" said Randy. "For getting your cousin to come and watch the baby. For you to wrap your breasts. Stop the milk. So you would have time to do your studies and travel with me?"

Fernanda said nothing. Started to get up, head turned towards the plaintive whimpering of the baby. Looked back at her husband. "I was wondering Randy. Do you think we could take the baby with us. And Constance? To watch the baby for us?"

"A second honeymoon complete with nanny and baby?" said Randy, setting down his juice. He didn't actually dislike Constance, with her wine bottle body – no waist – and her blocky, blunt face. Just found her a bit creepy with her constant talk of saints and her icon-painted prayer candles that she insisted on burning. "Somehow that doesn't sound very romantic."

"Paris is romantic," said Fernanda. "You've told me many times." The baby screamed. Randy watched as Fernanda unbuttoned her blouse and loosened the tight wrap strangling her breasts.

"I'll breastfeed the baby one last time," she said, leaving the dining room.

After a moment, Randy heard the baby go quiet. He took another bite of his *migas*. And had second thoughts about taking Fernanda to Paris. Nanny and baby or not, Paris was a dangerous city to visit. Because it *was* so romantic. And, yes, because his ex-mistress Julie still lived there.

4 Constance

The nanny's proper name was Constancia, though she preferred the Americanized version of Constance. Born in the US twenty years ago, she was largely raised across the border in Nuevo Laredo, Mexico, where life was cheaper. Even as a young girl, playing hand slap or pick up the pebbles, she realized, in comparison to the other girls, she hadn't the quickest wit, but she was OK with that. Her brain moved more like one of those freight trains crossing the border bridge, constant and sure, with illegals jumping on for a ride to the Promised Land.

"There," said Fernanda as the baby made her last little swallow and fell deep asleep. Constance watched as Fernanda lay her gently in the crib and covered her. "I have some good news for you," Fernanda said, smiling at Constance. "Randy told me that you could come with us to Paris. You and the baby. If you want."

"*Por supuesto*," said Constance. "I would love to come." She clasped Fernanda's hands a moment, her heart beating in her ears.

"You have your passport?"

"Yes."

"I just feel uncomfortable leaving the baby," explained Fernanda.

Constance adored Fernanda. Though not a blood cousin, she was as close to one as she might ever know. And unlike Randy, Fernanda said she appreciated Constance's extreme devotion to the Catholic Church, that she found this both comforting and touching.

"*Tu sabes*," Constance said, "they say the Crown of Thorns is held in the cathedral in Paris, at the Notre Dame Cathedral." She paced by the crib, all kinds of inspiration flowing into her. She was going with Fernanda to see the Crown. To touch the Crown! "Can you imagine? The True Crown. To touch it! All your sins, all your ills, would surely pass away. Poof."

Fernanda smiled and touched the top of Constance's head. "For those who believe," she said. "For ones like you."

Constance ran upstairs to her small room in the attic of the cabin, with its ceiling beams and small window overlooking the open mine. She glanced outside, saw the morning sun flash on the mine's mammoth quartz veins. She sat on her bed then and logged onto the laptop Randy had bought for her when she first came to stay with them - when he had caught sight of her old beat-up computer and said, "That won't do."

She signed onto the PEOPLE blog, and, trying to contain her emotion, typed as eruditely as she could her latest comment on the still active thread about Fernanda, entitled, Fernanda the Innocent.

"I have confirmation that Fernanda the Innocent is leaving for Paris. I have been invited to come as well, to be at her side, to attend what could be the second biggest event in the history of the Church. This may be the moment so many of us have been waiting for. Why do I say this? Think about it! Paris. Where the Crown of Thorns is kept. The Holy Crown that was on His Head when He was crucified. Think! She is going to the city where lies the Crown of Thorns!"

She clicked Send, sat back and waited for the comments – sure this post would launch an avalanche. She loved interacting with the world this way. She had never had such interaction with people back on the border. With people in person. Here on the internet she could dare to say what she truly believed. Here on the internet every voice was equal, every faceless person beautiful. Beautiful souls. Reaching out. Touching without touching. Everything was possible on the internet.

5 A Thorn in Ed's side

The Saint Anthony Chapel sits majestically just outside Pittsburgh, a white stone Catholic Church with twin bell towers topped with gold crosses, a church with the second largest collection of religious relics in the world, second only to the Vatican. On the third step of the building FBI agent Ed Pushkin felt white lightning traverse the left side of his chest. Heart attack? He was, after all, almost sixty, and a good twenty pounds overweight. But no: just a mystery pain, gone as quickly as it came, leaving in its wake the memory of Peru and that god-awful hike of ten thousand steps in the Andes keeping a tail on the suspect in his last case, Fernanda the Ripper. Fernanda the Beautiful. He'd almost lost his life on that hike, had suffered greatly. Requested a three month hiatus, to fully recover. When he'd returned to his old position with the FBI, they reassigned him. First a desk job. Then, finally, this new case, the burglary of Saint Anthony's, the case of the Holy Thorn. His veined aging hand grasped the cold door handle. He paused, wondered what Fernanda and her husband Randy and her crazy ex-boyfriend Chance were up to. He had to admit he

15

missed them. That had been a hell of a hike together. Would he ever experience such adventure and friendship again? Perhaps the saints whose pieces lay in gold boxes inside this church had some idea. Would let him know.

These were strange times. The tech bubble, now popped. The Catholic Church on the brink of bankruptcy for covering up sexual predator priests. Online communities forming, where rumors often trumped the truth. Were such happenings an indication of the End Times? He hadn't gone to church since his twenties. Didn't realize he would be so moved as he stood at the door to this one. Loneliness and dread flooded him. A sudden realization that he would end long before time did.

He pushed open the door. A smell of burning candles and something else, a rumor of long dead things. He stepped forward to the last row of wooden pews in the spacious church with its stained glass windows and Stations of the Cross exhibits along the wall. So much pain exhibited there, Christ suffering, over and over, endlessly, and no one to help him. The heavy door closed behind Ed with a firm click. Ed felt a tightening in the chest, felt as if the church, with its Christian imagery and relic-covered walls, was closing in on him, sealing him in like a tomb. A dark figure approached him.

"Welcome," said the middle-aged man in black robe and white collar. He had a crewcut that clashed with his soft features. "I'm Matthew, Father of the Saint Anthony parish."

"I'm FBI," said Ed. He fumbled for his badge. Rusty, he thought, I'm rusty at this.

"So you are here about ..."

"The stolen relic," Ed finished for him. "An old plant I believe?"

"You could call it that," said Father Matthew with a smile. "Actually though, a thorn. From the Crown of Thorns. It is one of our most cherished relics. Second only to our wood from the Cross itself." He turned, and Ed thought he moved a bit too gracefully in that robe, more like a woman than a man. "Let me give you a tour," he said, waving his arm.

They passed ceramic three-quarter size dioramas of Christ on the Cross. Ed never really appreciated the image of a man (a God?) being tortured to death. Yet he thought it was a pretty good metaphor for his own life: the torture of having to make a living, the torture of a wife gone mad with alzheimers. His had been a good long torture. Oh, he was in a foul mood this morning.

"We have over five thousand relics of the first and second class," said Father Matthew.

"First and second class?" said Ed.

"First class being a part of a saint's body or instruments of Christ's Passion. Second class being something the saints owned, or something used to torture them," explained Father Matthew. His eyes twinkled, which annoyed Ed. "Third class is something that has touched a first or second class relic."

They stopped before a display covered with gold lockets, each with a hair, a splinter of bone, a tooth from a saint.

"So if I touch one of these I would be a third class relic?"

"If you want to think of yourself as such," said Father Matthew, smiling again.

"The younger agents at the office already do," said Ed. He couldn't help but smile back. Father Matthew opened a locket and held it out so Ed could touch the old fragment of bone nestled inside.

"Does it have magic power?" asked Ed, reaching with a finger and tapping the bone. "Does magic power get transferred to me by touch?"

"The Bible says that even the touch of Saint Peter's shadow cured the sick," said Father Matthew. "Magic power? Yes. I suppose you could call Faith that."

"Which saint is it from?" Ed asked.

"Saint Jude," said Father Matthew. "The saint of hopeless causes."

"Well chosen!" said Ed. "So each saint has a specialty?"

"Most do, and a feast day, his is October 28th," said Father Matthew. He put up the relic of Saint Jude and brought down another locket from the wall. "Hair from Saint Philomena. She is also good for lost causes."

Ed touched the hair as well. Felt his own hair rise on the back of his neck. "How did she die?" he asked.

"Beautifully," said Father Matthew. "The Emperor Diocletian saw her near the baths one day and chose her to be his new bride. She refused, telling him that she had dedicated her virginity to Christ. He had her arrested and flogged, hoping that torture would change her mind."

"I guess in those days they didn't realize that flowers and chocolate could move a woman's heart," said Ed.

"She had disrespected the Emperor," said Father Matthew. "So the torture was part punishment and part persuasion." He sounded like he was settling into a story he'd told many times, his voice took on the rhythm of a sermon. "She was whipped brutally, poor Philomena, but still she would not agree to wed the Emperor. So Diocletian had an anchor tied to her neck and she was thrown into the river. By some miracle, she surfaced, free of the anchor. Exasperated with this girl who would not concede and worse yet, she would not die, he had his men drill her with arrows. Yet not a single arrow found her heart. Standing there, out of breath, dripping wet, scarred and bloody from the flogging, arrows sticking out of her chest, she raised her head and spoke in a whisper of her undying faith in Jesus Christ. A whisper that shook the Emperor to the bone. He commanded his men to cut off her head, and so she died, still true to our Lord."

"Wow," said Ed.

The Father nodded. "Her relics over the centuries have produced many miracles."

That's not a beautiful way to die, thought Ed. That's a horrible way to die. And he had touched her hair, had received her insane stubbornness through that touch. Or something worse.

Ed felt sleepy. That must explain his bad mood. Kept waking up last night. And his glass eye was itchy.

"We venerate these relics," said Father Matthew, "as they remind us of the many holy men and women who lived and died for Christ our Savior."

They moved from the wall of lockets to a glass display case of trophy-looking treasures. A hole in the case was taped over. Father Matthew unlocked the case.

"A smash and grab," said Ed.

"A smash, yes, but not so much a grab as a careful extraction," said Father Matthew.

"These are our reliquaries. Gold and silver plated, decorated with semi-precious gems. Here is the one that held the missing thorn. Dates back to 1600."

"Don't touch it," said Ed.

"Oh the police have already dusted for prints. There were none of interest."

"But wait," said Ed. "How much would you say this trophy, this reliquary, is worth?"

"To me, it is priceless," said Father Matthew.

"But to the pawnbroker, downtown Pittsburgh - how much is it worth to him?"

"The frame is gold-plated. Worth at least a thousand dollars," said Father Matthew. "If you found the right buyer, someone interested in the relic more than in the gold, it could be worth much more."

"Interesting," said Ed. "And they didn't steal it."

"No. Only the Holy Thorn."

Ed rubbed his unshaven chin.

"And how much is that thorn worth?" he asked.

"The Holy Thorn is priceless," said Father Matthew.

"For you, I understand, but?"

"If I had to put a price tag on it," said Father Matthew. "I would price the Thorn close to a million dollars."

Ed did a double-take. Had to pause and let that sink in. A million dollar thorn. First class relic. And they didn't take the container, whose gold could have been melted down and been sold risk free. His interest was piqued, his detective spirit awakened.

"And all these other relics and reliquaries here, how much would you say they are all worth?"

"I'm sorry, I don't like to think of all these marvels in terms of money," said Father Matthew.

"You're attached to all this, aren't you?" said Ed. "Personally attached."

"They are my children," said Father Matthew. "The real value of the relics is not in dollars. One can make that mistake, but think about it. How much is a baby's laugh worth? How much the smile of a lover? How much is it worth, our freedom to worship? Not all things can be valued properly if all you think of is their monetary value."

"I understand, Father," said Ed, feeling a bit as if he were in Sunday school. "OK. Give me some background then on the thorn. So I can understand better the motivation of stealing it and leaving the container."

Father Matthew took a deep breath and let it out slowly. He

then explained that if Ed really wanted to know about the Thorn, they would need to start at the beginning. Start with Emperor Constantine, and the foundation of his new Roman-Byzantium capital Constantinople, in the year 300.

"No," said Ed, cutting him off. "I don't mean for you to go that far back."

"But in this case I think it might be helpful. To understand the importance of the Holy Thorn and why someone might steal it."

"OK, then," said Ed. "Can we sit down?"

"Of course, sorry, where are my manners?" Ed sat in the first pew, leaving no space on the end so Father Matthew would be forced to go around him and sit facing his good eye.

Father Matthew continued. "In building a new capital in what is now Istanbul, Emperor Constantine found himself in a power struggle with Rome and the Catholic hierarchy based there. For he wanted to move not just the political power from Rome but also the religious power. To that end, he sent his mother, Saint Helena, to Jerusalem, to find what relics she could and bring them, and the power they represented, to Constantinople."

Ed glanced at the man, then looked straight ahead, continuing to listen as intently as his mood would allow.

"Saint Helena's search was blessed, and she found many relics, the most important being the Cross, the nails and the Crown of Thorns."

"She found the Cross? Three hundred years after the crucifixion?"

"Three hundred years after Christ's Passion, yes," said Father Matthew. "Certain people realized the importance of the event, and saved what we call relics."

"Souvenirs," said Ed.

"If you wish. These people of the faith in Jerusalem, these souvenir hunters as you say, brought Saint Helena to the three crosses that had been in their family for generations. The crucifixion crosses of the two thieves and of Christ. So how was she to pick the right cross to take back with her to Constantinople? Any idea, Mr FBI?"

"No clue," said Ed.

"She had a woman who was deathly ill touch each of the crosses. The ill woman touched the first one, and nothing happened. The second, nothing still. But when she touched the third cross ..."

"She was cured."

It was a guess on Ed's part, but Father Matthew nodded.

"Yes, she was," said Father Matthew. "On the spot. That is how Saint Helena knew she had the right cross."

"And the Crown of Thorns?"

"She found it, the woven Crown of Thorns, but was not allowed to take it from the church that held it in Jerusalem. Only a few Holy Thorns was she allowed to take. The Crown of Thorns itself remained in Jerusalem for another seven hundred years, brought to Constantinople for save-keeping in 1063. Two hundred years later, near the collapse of the Byzantine Empire, Emperor Baldwin II gave the Crown of Thorns to the king of France. Only he forgot to mention that he had pawned the Crown to Venetian money lenders."

"Aw, so relics do get pawned," said Ed.

"A shameful episode," said Father Matthew. He sat quietly, rubbing his signet ring. A chirp and desperate flapping of wings made them both look up. A bird, high in a dark corner of the church interior, was trying to find the way out. "After a day or two I'll find him on the floor, exhausted."

Ed felt uneasy and wanted to leave, before he too was found on the floor. But he needed a little more info. "So the king of France paid the pawn ticket?"

"Louis the IX paid the debt and built Saint Chapelle in Paris as a reliquary to house the Crown. After the French Revolution, the Crown was moved to Notre Dame. Over time, Thorns were plucked from the Crown and given to kings, who passed them on to favorite knights, and to holy men and holy places around the world. These

Thorns changed hands over the centuries. We were lucky to acquire our own a hundred years ago."

"And now it's gone," said Ed.

"But you will find it for us," said Father Matthew. "Now that you have the magic power of the saints on your side."

"Oh yes," said Ed. His phone rang, making him jump. These FBI issue cellphones were the latest thing, yet Ed hated the idea that his boss could call him anytime, anywhere.

"Excuse me, Father." He got up and stepped a few yards away.

Another thorn robbery. And a murder to boot. The British Museum. Ed listened in silence as his boss said he needed to visit England – specifically, Waddesdon Manor, the Rothschild estate. He also needed to call INTERPOL, who suspected a European or Middle-East connection, before he caught that flight. Ed listened, nodding, and when the call ended he sighed, putting away his phone.

"Thank you, Father. Looks like I'm off to other lands to catch your crook."

"May the saints guide you, my son."

Ed walked back past the ceramic parade of crucifixions, of the torture of Christ.

"Son," Father Matthew called after him.

Ed stopped, turned halfway. "Yes?"

"Your eye. Don't worry. It looks good. Quite natural."

"Thanks," Ed said. "Father?"

"Yes."

"The thorn. Would you recognize it, if I did find it?"

"Yes, I would," said the Father, with surprising conviction. "I'll be praying for you."

Ed opened the chapel door and stepped out into the chilly air. He didn't really feel up to a flight across the ocean. Felt jet-lagged already. Wished he were back in the Andes despite what happened, despite the torture of those never-ending Inca steps. Or better yet, to be back in Russia with Marina, the friend he'd made when visiting Siberia, on his hiatus from the FBI. Anywhere but on a mission to track down a missing thorn. Two thorns now. Relics of the first class, among other relics of bone and hair from countless saints who apparently all died horrible deaths. Maybe he was destined to be an unknown saint himself, he wondered. Tortured to death by the inanities of life. But who would venerate *his* bones?

6 Into the eye of the storm

Well of course it was raining - a cold drizzle whipped by the North Sea breeze. *And* they'd screwed up his orders. HQ or INTERPOL. Or both. Because when Ed arrived at the opulent Waddesdon Manor built by Baron Ferdinand Rothschild in the 1870s, it was only to be told that the Holy Thorn Reliquary, the object of inquiry for which he'd flown a thousand miles, hadn't been in the manor in over a hundred years. It had been offered as a bequest to the British Museum when the old Baron died. So none of the current staff at the place knew anything about it, or the robbery of the thorn. Dead end.

But would he like to visit Lord Rothschild's fifteen thousand bottles of old wine in the cellar of the Waddesdon Manor?

"Only if I'm allowed to down a bottle," said Ed.

"No, sorry, this is Lord Rothschild's private collection," explained the clerk who was still waiting for Ed to pay entrance to the faux-chateau turned museum.

"He's saving all that wine for himself?" said Ed. "The bugger!" He turned away, pulled out his phone. Called HQ and got the details right this time. Or the right details. Chief Inspector Mullins would meet him at the entrance to the British Museum, downtown London. He grabbed a "Who are the Rothschilds?" brochure on his way out, and caught a taxi. During the long ride back he read about the Rothschild family - how they turned an antique business started in the 1700s into a worldwide investment banking empire. One of the Rothschild's, Sir Evelyn De Rothschild, was the richest man in the world. Worth at least twenty billion dollars. Most of this rich family, it appeared, for the last two hundred years, were collectors. Had spent millions on trinkets, old furniture and relics. Ed wondered how some people had so much money, money to waste, when he always had so little.

"Ed?" the uniformed woman said, appearing from behind one of the massive tarnished columns at the top of the stairs of the British Museum. "I'm Chief Inspector Mullins."

Ed almost took a step back, then caught himself, realizing just in time that a step back would mean a hard fall down the stone steps. Without stepping back then - standing a little too close - he looked over this late forties, early fifties, still striking Jamaican-looking woman with brown skin and dark freckles on her cheeks and nose.

Her inquisitive eyes widened.

"I like a woman in uniform," Ed said. "How did you recognize me, though?"

"You dress like," she started to say, then caught herself. "Lucky guess. I guess." She gave him a sideways smile.

My eye, thought Ed. She must have heard the story, how I lost my eye.

"What kind of accent is that?" he asked.

"Yours or mine?"

That made him smile, despite feeling self-conscious.

"Mine is American," he said.

"Mine is South London," she said, leading him inside the old regal building.

Ed humphed.

"No ticket counter?" he said.

"All the national museums are free," she replied. "Thanks to the Labour party. Initiated just in time for your visit."

He liked the place immediately then. So few museums in the states were free anymore.

CI Mullins led him past the inside circular court where the restaurant and souvenir shop were situated, up three flights to a room full of Japanese paintings. He liked the simplicity of style and color in the paintings. So much emotion, loneliness, eternity, told in single strokes. He paused, taking in his surroundings, when CI Mullins said, "Sorry. I always get lost when I come here. I think the Rothschild relics are this way."

A long high-ceilinged hall, then down a flight of royal stairs, and they arrived before the prize pieces of the Rothschild bequest. A curious collection of paintings and gold carvings, triptychs and wooden prayer nuts that opened to show tiny carved Passions of Christ. And last but not least, the Holy Thorn Reliquary. A small beautiful gold box trimmed with tiny white ceramic angels and purple gemstones and perfect pearls, with a front compartment for the Holy Thorn covered by a pane of clear quartz.

"You see," CI Mullins said, "inside, before the Christ figure, the missing thorn."

"No I don't see it," said Ed.

"I mean, you see it is missing," said CI Mullins.

"Right. I don't see it," said Ed.

They looked at each other. He wondered if she was trying to be difficult. She looked away, stifling a laugh.

"Who was killed?" Ed asked after a long silence.

"A night watchman. Would you like to see the spot?"

"No," said Ed. Another long silence.

"They didn't take the reliquary," she said. "Only the thorn. That has to mean something."

"Means they were willing to kill for it," said Ed.

"Look," she said, then hesitated. "I ... I have a theory ..."

He waited. She looked about nervously.

"Go on," he told her.

"I have this theory ... but I'd like to tell you off the record. A bit later, maybe. Have you had your lunch?"

"Nope," said Ed.

"Let's go down to the Queen's walk, along the river, and get a bite," she said, brightening up. "Your treat."

Ed's first thought was to turn her down. Normally he liked to lunch alone. But he knew that would be impolite. And anyway she had a theory. Off the record or not, he should hear her out.

"OK," he said, "but my treat."

"That's what I said. Your treat." She started down the stairway past a pack of Chinese girl scouts in brown shorts and high white socks.

"If you insist. Wait, did you say, my treat?" He followed her, watched how she held herself high, how her hips rotated with each step. Raise your eyes, he whispered to himself. You're too old for her.

On the river walk Ed was surprised to see street musicians and mimes and acrobatic performers. A strung-out circus. With food trucks and wagons as well as restaurants for the British lunch crowd.

She went up to one of the wagons that said "Laughing Halibut's" and ordered fish and chips. Ed watched in horror as the man poured vinegar over both the fish and the French fries. Oh well.

She passed him his paper basket and they settled on a bench looking out across the Thames.

The Thames River reminded Ed of the Mississippi. Same kind of majesty. Businessmen in suits and businesswomen in dresses, as well as tourists with kids, mingled along the walk under an ironwork bridge.

"So, did you ever find Jack the Ripper?" Ed asked.

CI Mullins choked on her fish. "Me? Personally?" she managed to say after a drink of her bottled water. "Why would you ask me such a question?"

"We have a similar case," Ed said. "The FBI. The Federal Police in Peru. Police in India. Only it's a woman. She mutilates and kills men. In Delhi they call her Kali the Ripper. In the states we call her Fernanda the Ripper." Ed jammed another French fry into his mouth. Tasted the vinegar. "I worked the case for a while."

CI Mullins puzzled over what he said. "And you think this Holy Thorns case is related in some way?"

"I wonder," he said, and took another bite of his deep-fried fish. Excellent fish, actually. The vinegar was a nice touch for both the fish and the fries. "So tell me your theory."

He watched as she stared at the huge spinning wheel across the river. She reminded him of a little girl, longing for a ride.

"Quite an attraction," he said.

"Have you been on the London Eye?" she asked. "Just opened."

"No. My first trip to England."

"Then you must come," and she took his hand. Led him to the circular stairwell of the bridge. His hand in hers unnerved him, they were after all professionals, relative strangers, and neither one a child, and though she did let go after a minute, he was left with both a fuzziness of the normal boundary between them and, despite himself, a childish eagerness to board the giant wheel with her. To enter the Eye and see what he could see.

7 Fans?

"Who are those girls?" Randy said to Chance as they walked through the mounds of dirt and red-stained clay clods mixed with chunks of white quartz, tailings from the crystal mine they owned. Of all the rockhounds that had paid $10 each to dig in the tailings for loose crystals and small clusters, these four teenage girls weren't digging. They just sat cross-legged on a mound, heads down, hands teepee-ed, in a kind of trance.

"Who cares," said Chance. "As long as they paid to dig." Chance was Randy's old high school buddy, and Fernanda's ex-boyfriend. (How they came to live next to each other, on a mine in Arkansas, was a long story. Suffice it to say that fate wanted it that way.) Chance worked the mine while Randy provided, when needed, cash from his programming job to fix the heavy equipment, the excavator and the dump truck. Chance was the brawn (and handsome to boot), Randy the brains, and Fernanda the beauty in the partnership.

"But weren't they here yesterday as well?" said Randy. "What are they up to?"

"Man, if you're so interested, why don't you just ask them?"

Randy was shy, despite his profession as a consultant who traveled the world meeting customers, and dodged talking to new people whenever he could. But he forced himself to walk over to the teenagers.

"Excuse me," he said loudly enough to make the girls jump.

They stared at him.

"Can I help you?" Randy said. "Do you need instruction on crystal digging?"

"No," said the tallest in the group, a blond. She stood atop the mound, towering over Randy. "We're not here for the crystals."

"You're not?" said Randy, shading his eyes as he looked up to her.

"Then why are you here?" asked Chance. "There's nothing here but crystals and dirt."

"Fernanda the Innocent is here," she said. "Don't deny it."

Randy looked at Chance, who raised his thick black eyebrows.

"Do you think we could meet her?" said another of the girls, the cute one with a pixie haircut. "Yes, please," chimed in the others.

"You want to talk to Fernanda?" said Randy.

"Please?" said the tall blond, rubbing her hands together as she stepped down off the mound. "We've come so far. All the way from LA. To receive her blessing."

8 A new congregation

"What does this one do?" asked Constance as she pawed at Fernanda's herbs, which were spread out on the bed along with her clothes for the trip to Paris. They were leaving on Saturday, so there was much packing to do and little time.

"That one is ayahuasca," said Fernanda. "Taken as a tea, it helps one talk with the spirits. To do divinations."

"Have you taken it yourself?"

"No," said Fernanda. "My teacher, Paro, says I am not ready. That I might draw the wrong spirits, the dark ones. But I've seen him take it. I've sat at one of his divinations."

When Fernanda bent over to put clothes into the open suitcase, Constance grabbed a handful of the herb and stuffed it in her pants' pocket. She loved the idea of talking with spirits, not evil spirits of course, but with the holy ones, the saints. She longed for their advice. Concerning Fernanda. Was she truly the One? Constance struggled with this question. How she could help Fernanda, and thereby help the Church?

Already divided into so many confusing denominations, into Protestant and Methodist, Lutheran and Evangelical, Eastern Orthodox and Mennonite, the Original True Church was losing thousands if not millions of believers every year. And the recent news stories of priest molestations of children and cover-ups by "Holy" ones who did not want the Church to lose power, who did not want to lose power themselves, certainly weren't helping the matter. Christ's teachings had inspired humanity for two thousand years, but now the faint echo of his words, the long ago example of his suffering, has become muted with time. What was needed was a Second Coming to revive the Church, to reunite all the churches into the One Church. What was needed was a new Messiah. Constance was sure of that. And what if Fernanda was the One? And why shouldn't the new Messiah be a woman?

As if in answer, the front door opened and Chance's voice boomed out, "Fernanda! Some girls are here to worship you!"

9 Good intentions

"So who do you think is behind the two stolen thorns?" said Ed to CI Mullins as they stood, a little too close for his comfort, in the slow moving line of the giant London Carousel.

"Six stolen thorns and one murder," she said. "Probably more."

"More thorn thefts?" asked Ed, noticing how her eyes crinkled, but in a nice way. As if she had smiled and laughed a lot over the years. "Or more murders?"

"Thorns," she told him. They shuffled forward as the line moved. "I've heard theft reports from Germany, Spain, and Italy."

"News to me," said Ed. "But I'm not surprised. I think sometimes my boss gives me as few details as possible. On purpose."

She shot him a double-take at that pronouncement.

"And your theory?" he asked. "Who is doing this?"

"Wait," she said, pointing to the clear pods as they slowly rotated around the white-spoked axle. So he waited, silently. Once he accidentally brushed against her back side, thinking she had moved ahead when she had not. He started to apologize, but he wasn't really sorry. Was a nice feeling, to brush up against this woman of the world, this leader of men. This middle-aged uniformed female with her secret theory. Her conspiracy that she was only willing to share with Mr FBI, Mr INTERPOL, with Ed and Ed alone.

They were on the platform now, and the next clear pod, shaped like a giant glass eye, silently pulled into position before them. CI Mullins showed her badge to the London Eye staff in charge of loading the pods and told them that she and Ed would be riding by themselves.

They stepped in, the clear door sealed and the pod began its slow circular climb into the London sky.

Ed waited, watched CI Mullins stand in front of the panorama unfolding before them as they rose higher and higher. The river, the Queen's walk, Big Ben and parliament. Over there a bit farther was the theatre district, with its clubs and the best live actors in the world. Was CI Mullins one of those actors? Taking him for a ride?

"So?" he asked.

She turned and faced him. Such a darkly intelligent, interesting face, with the freckles suggesting the girl she once was. "This has to be off the record," she told him, "because if my superiors found out, if the public found out, and I was wrong, my career would be over. I would be ruined."

He showed concern, nodded. "I understand." He did not ask her why she trusted him. Was it his glass eye? He hoped it was his honest soul visible through his real eye.

"I believe the church is behind the thefts, behind the murder," she said. "Maybe even the Pope."

He tried not to smile. So, she was crazy after all. "OK," he said. The giant glass eye in which they rode neared the summit of its arc. On a clear day he wondered if you could see all the way to the English Channel. To Normandy. But it was not a clear day. Drizzle began to shroud the glass. Nothing was clear anymore.

"You think I am crazy," she said.

He turned sideways to her, looked down. Falling through the floor of the pod, from this height, would mean sure death, even if you somehow made the river and not the concrete below. "I don't know what to think. Yet. Please continue, CI Mullins."

"Phoebe," she said. "My name is Phoebe."

"Please Phoebe, continue."

"These are thorns from the Crown of Thorns, yes?" she asked.

"They are supposed to be, yes," he agreed.

"Which is kept in the Notre Dame Cathedral. So I made a discreet call to a colleague of mine in the Prefecture of Paris, if something might be up with the Crown of Thorns. He did a couple of calls himself, and discovered that the Crown of Thorns is currently being restored."

"Restored?" asked Ed. He rubbed his chin. "As in, put missing thorns back on the Crown?"

"I would assume so," she said. "Such restoration would have to be blessed by the highest authorities in the church. Think of the risk."

"So you think the Pope authorized this restoration? Gave his blessing to get more thorns, no matter what it took?"

"Not exactly," she said. "I think the Catholic Church is rich. Richer than you and I can imagine. And they are currently getting disgraceful press. With the dreadful priest thing and the cover-ups. They are very much in need of a win. Of good publicity. So I think they came up with this idea for a positive press release – 'Church restores the Crown of Thorns. Come see the marvelous relic!' Maybe do a world tour with it."

"But why steal the thorns, why murder a guard?" Ed asked. The pod started down now, everything small growing larger. "Why not just buy them?"

"It's complicated," Phoebe said. "First of all, no one with an authenticated thorn would be willing to sell it. They just wouldn't. Second, Church law makes it a sin to buy or sell first class relics like the thorns. So no amount of money is necessarily going to get them a single authenticated thorn for their planned restoration. The church authorities know that, the Pope's staff knows that, so they pick a certain company, a certain individual, who they trust to be discreet about getting the thorns. Who they trust to do whatever it takes to make it happen."

"Wow," said Ed. "And who do you think then they hired?"

"We need to go to Paris," she said, biting her lower lip in a girlish way. "To find out."

"We?" said Ed. "Paris?"

"If we want to find who is behind the thorn robberies, we have to find out who the Church hired to restore the Crown." She really believed what she was telling him, she wasn't acting, he could tell.

The glass pod came to a crawl at the platform. They stepped off.

"Paris?" said Ed again, as they stepped down to the sidewalk. "For how long?"

"I plan to take a week vacation," she told him. "Go in an unofficial capacity, yes? I have no authority there, and I repeat, I can't let anyone in my office know who I suspect is behind all this. But you have authority, Ed, don't you? No matter where you go. Being with INTERPOL."

Ed looked her straight in the eyes.

"Why do you want to risk so much on this case? Why risk your whole career on one case?"

"Look Ed. I'm nearing retirement." He noticed the fatigue in her face when she said it. "Most of the cases I've worked all these years have put me to sleep. Or made me sick. But this case, this case feels different. I sense it, in my heart. I think this case matters, Ed. Really matters."

Ed considered the Chief Inspector's explanation. Was a nice explanation but still her theory was off the wall. Crazy. On the other hand, a week with this particular lady in a romantic city like Paris was not a bad proposal. "I like the idea," he told her, finally. "Let's go to Paris and get to the bottom of this."

10 What could she say?

In Arkansas, at the quartz mine, on the porch of the second cabin built on the premises (the first cabin belonging to Chance and his wife Crystal), Fernanda stood barefoot looking down at the four girls who had come all the way from Los Angeles to meet her. Constance stood behind and to her right, next to the screen door, having persuaded Chance and Randy to stay inside and watch the baby.

"Can I help you?" said Fernanda, leaning forward in her summer dress, careful not to slide her feet and catch a splinter from the planks. Beyond the four girls standing in the gravel lay the tailings, large mounds of dirt brought up each morning with a dump truck from the mine. A few rockhounds sat on the sides of the dark mounds clawing at the dirt with screwdrivers and pronged weeders, searching for loose crystals. Beyond the mine lay forest and rolling hills.

Constance wondered what Fernanda must be thinking. Would she take this opportunity to give her first sermon?

"We came for your blessing," said the tall blond, inching a bit closer to the porch steps, a bit closer to her new idol. She stuck her hands into the front pockets of her jeans. A hummingbird zipped in front of her, paused a second at the flowerbed, then disappeared.

Constance moved forward, she wanted to see Fernanda's face. To read better how she was taking in this first meeting with her followers. Her disciples.

A muffled hum rose and fell as bumble bees swarmed the blue plastic trash bin, across the way, filled with empty, sweetly-sticky soda cans and crumpled salty chip bags.

Fernanda gently waved a bee from her face - a remarkably friendly brown face which seemed to glow. "Of course you have my blessing," she said. She stepped down and gave each of them a hug, sending them into tears.

Constance, filled with emotion, dropped to her knees next to Fernanda and asked for her blessing as well.

"Dear Constancia," said Fernanda, touching her lightly on the head, "it is you who bless me with all your help."

Constance grabbed hold of her legs. "Thank you, thank you." She released Fernanda, and felt a wave of warmth throughout her body, as if her soul had been bathed.

"Tell us, Fernanda the Innocent," said one of the girls – the one who looked like a pixie, "please tell us how to live our lives."

"Yes," said another, "should we become nuns or missionaries or ...?"

"Fernanda the Innocent?" said Fernanda, puzzling, for a moment, over the expression. "Is this about the PEOPLE article?"

"Oh no," said the blond. "We only read that later."

"Later?"

"Yes," said the pixie, "we first heard about you weeks ago on FaceSpace. There was a link to PEOPLE too. Everyone is talking about you. How you're overflowing with love. How you were born to be sacrificed. Just like Jesus."

"Just like Jesus, only better," said the blond. "Because you are a woman."

Constance jumped to catch Fernanda when she saw her sway. But she only swayed a moment, righted herself, and shook her head.

"I'm not so sure I was born to be sacrificed," said Fernanda. "Despite what everyone tells me."

Constance watched as Fernanda measured the moment, measured her words. A muffled cry, the baby, sounded from the open door of the large cabin, and Fernanda turned.

"Please," said the tall blond. "Don't go! Tell us what to do with our lives."

"Live them," said Fernanda. She started up the steps, then paused, her hand on the rail, her long black hair shining silver in the sun. She said to the girls, "I am a simple woman. That is what I do. I live my life." She met each of their teary eyes, raised her right hand in a kind of second blessing and said, "And be mindful, girls. If nothing else, be mindful of others." She disappeared into the gloom of the house, leaving Constance with the sun in her eyes.

11 Like wildfire

By the time Constance sat down to the internet, there were already two different versions of Fernanda's first sermon doing the rounds. The first version, posted on PEOPLE's site and propagated from a FaceSpace write-up, ran:

Do as I do. Live simple lives. Be mindful of others, for mindfulness is critical in understanding your place in the world.

The second version, less viral, went like this:

As the miner digs in dirt for crystals and gold, so should you dig in the dirt of your life for precious moments. Your life can be like a mine, full, if you will only try to be more mind full.

Rather than post still another version of Fernanda's words, Constance chose to write a firsthand account of how Fernanda struck her, with a little help from the new search site Google and with a lot of help from spell check:

I stood not three feet from Fernanda the Innocent when she gave her first sermon. Her face glowed with the Spirit of God, and all who listened were transformed by her words. She was the personification of Saint Sophia (Wisdom) and all three of her daughters Faith, Hope and Love.

Remember the story of Saint Sophia and her daughters? The early Christian family was brought before the mighty Roman emperor Hadrian. The emperor offered to adopt the first daughter, twelve year old Faith, if only she would deny Christ and worship Artemis, the Roman Goddess of virginity, of the hunt and of the moon. When she refused Hadrian had Faith stripped and flogged. He asked her again to give up God and again she refused, so he had her breasts cut off. And all were amazed for she bled milk, not blood. The emperor scoffed and told his men to grill her, then boil her. She sang softly to God through all this, so the emperor gave up trying to convert Faith and simply had them cut off her head.

The second daughter, ten year old Hope, was similarly tortured, and similarly obstinate. They suspended her and raked her body with hooks, tearing off her flesh. "Simply say your god is false and you will be free of all this," the emperor told her. But she refused, her bloody wounds smelling of red roses. Furious, the emperor had them sever her head as well.

Tiny Love, only nine, was first stretched on a wheel until all her members were pulled from their sockets. Would she declare Goddess Artemis to be great, and save herself? No, Love refused. So they placed her in a red hot furnace. But she came out untouched and defiant. The torturers set to work with drills then, small and large, boring into her body. But she did not die and still refused to admit she loved a false god. Finally, as with her two sisters, they chopped off her head.

Their mother Sophia was allowed to bury their bodies. She lay down three days and nights next to their graves, heartbroken, and passed then herself to our Lord.

I swear, as I stood there not three feet from Fernanda the Innocent as she gave her first sermon, I swear I recognized in her the Spirit of all four of them, of Saint Sophia, of Faith, of Hope and especially of little Love.

God Bless Fernanda.

12 A dab of syrup

Fernanda could not sleep. Or would not. For she knew the nightmare awaited. The one where headless figures and bodiless heads circled her, crowded her, whispered that she must be sacrificed. That she was destined to become one of them.

Dios mio!

Fernanda trembled. Wanted to cry. Four girls had come today asking for a blessing. From her! *Que cosa!* She was the one in need of a blessing. She was the one that needed protection. From spirits. From nightmares. From life itself.

How could she stop the nightmare? How could she convince the spirits they had picked the wrong woman? She got up from Randy's side and checked the baby, who slept the deep sleep of the innocent. Then Fernanda puttered about the house, silently, like a ghost whose soul cannot reach the other side. Only the occasional floor creak gave notice of her restless passing. Finally the morning sun peaked through cracks in the curtains, biting her eyes. She lay down again by Randy's side, just as he began to stir

"I'm hungry for pancakes," he said.

"Ask Constance," she told him. "I want to rest a few more minutes." And she fell deeply asleep.

"They're out there," said Chance. He'd helped himself into the house, and now stepped into the small dining room where the family sat eating.

"Who?" asked Randy.

"More of Fernanda's admirers."

Randy got up and took a peek out the front window. "A good dozen. And not the same as yesterday."

"No," said Chance. "Appears word has spread." He sat down and helped himself to a pancake, smothering it with butter and syrup. He took a bite. "Mmmm. Hey you look good and baggy-eyed this morning," he said to Fernanda.

"Thanks," she said, adjusting the baby in her arms. "I was too excited about the trip last night to sleep."

"Poor you," said Constance, bringing a bottle of warmed milk from the kitchen. She handed the bottle to Fernanda, who teased the rubber nipple between little Rocky's lips. The baby took the nipple and slowly began to suck.

"She's drinking," whispered Fernanda.

"I told you she would," said Constance. "A dab of syrup does wonders."

After breakfast they cleaned up, gathered their luggage, and bid goodbye to Chance.

"Keep an eye on things for us," said Randy.

"Sure," said Chance. "Though you picked a hell of a time to leave. We've never had so many paying customers at the mine. I tell them it's ten dollars to dig in the tailings, whether you dig or not, and they don't blink an eye. Fernanda is quite a draw."

They stepped outside, and it was twenty people who surrounded them now.

"Fernanda! Fernanda the Innocent!" the cry went up. "Bless us Fernanda! Please bless us!"

What could she do? She told Randy to put the luggage in the car, had Constance hold the baby. She stepped down from the porch into the crowd.

"How can I help you?" she asked.

"Bless me, Fernanda," said a young man with a crewcut and an earring in his nose.

She reached out and he stepped into her embrace. She released him and he stumbled back, his eyes expressing wonder. He tried to speak but could not.

One by one she touched them all. This seemed to calm them, and satisfy the urge that had brought them to the mine.

Randy came up to her and said, "We have to leave now. We have a long drive to the airport. Paris awaits."

Fernanda gave a little wave to the people that had come to see her. She started towards the car where stood Constance with the baby.

"Wait," asked a woman in a long plain dress. Her face showed the stress of chronic illness. "How many times should I pray each day? How many times before God hears me?"

"Yes, how many times should we pray?" voiced another.

Fernanda stopped. Why did they think she knew the answer to such questions? Were they testing her, trying to trap her?

She faced the woman, noticing as she did a sparkle from the ground. A clear crystal. She bent over, grabbed it and held the crystal up. She wiggled the crystal back and forth in her fingers, so that it caught the rays of the sun and sparkled.

"Look," she said. "No matter how it appears, the crystal's spark is not her own." With that she walked away, got in the car and they drove out of the mine, passing a long line of cars coming in. Cars full of people wishing to see Fernanda, people traveling from near and far to speak with her and receive her blessing.

"*Que cosa!*" said Fernanda, moving down in her seat, trying to hide from all the pleading faces in the passing car windows. "What a thing to happen to me!"

13 Under the sea, the cold cold sea

"I didn't mean to hurt your feelings, ol' man," said CI Mullins, in a dress, on her vacation project, adjusting herself in the seat of the Eurostar. The train would take thirty minutes to cross under the English channel, then another hour, running across the open fields of northwest France, to reach Paris.

"Oh now I'm an old man?" Ed said, across from her, pretending hurt.

"No," said CI Mullins. "It's just an expression. Like *The ol' Man and the Sea*. That book."

"It was *The Old Man and the Sea*," said Ed. "About an *old* man."

"I don't think so," said CI Mullins. "Anyway, I just asked about your eye so I can stop wondering how you lost it."

Ed thought what to tell her.

"A shaman on the Inca Trail trepanned through my eye to remove a tumor," said Ed. "Used a hallucinogenic as the anesthetic."

CI Mullins' eyes widened. She leaned close to Ed, studied his eye. Then she pulled back and shook her pretty head.

"OK if you don't want to tell me the truth, how it happened, that's fine," she said. "I won't ask again."

"But I'm telling the truth," protested Ed.

"And I'm a blue-eyed blond from Scandinavia," she said. She took out the Guardian, opened it at random, and pretended to read.

Ed growled. This woman got under his skin too easily. Maybe this trip, this goose chase to Paris after a thief with a thorn fetish, maybe this wasn't the best idea he ever had. Or rather, that she had ever had.

He sat in silence until the silence became too loud to bear. He broke that silence, asked her a hurtful question himself.

"Do you have something against the Church?" he said. "This theory of yours that the Catholic Church is behind the thorn thefts and the murder, this isn't some kind of attempt to get revenge, is it? You weren't touched by a priest when you were young?"

CI Mullins choked. Took out her bottle of water and drank a swig. Coughed. Then she narrowed her eyes at Ed.

"I was raised Protestant," she said, tapping a finger on the arm rest. "And no to your questions. Like you, I am sure, I go where the facts point me. And in this case, the facts point to the Holy Crown.

To the Cathedral of Notre Dame. As you admitted yourself."

"And so here we find ourselves," said Ed. "On this train under the sea. Feeling out each other."

"Is that what you're trying to do to me, ol' man?" she said, her expression lightening. "Trying to feel me up?"

She laughed, and he laughed too. He did so enjoy looking into those crinkly eyes of hers. Liked the constellation of dark stars on her face. Mustn't like her too much, he warned himself. For where could that go?

The train came out of the tunnel like a rat and picked its way through a maze of tracks, through an industrial area, the outskirts of a city, where it transformed into a pony galloping over rolling hills, past forests and stone farmsteads built in the middle ages.

He relaxed, the idyllic French countryside soothing him. He wondered if Paris would live up to the hype.

They got off at the end of the line, at the Gare du Nord train station, and took a taxi from there to the city center where CI Mullins had arranged their lodgings. What beautiful architecture, Ed had to admit, as the taxi plied wide tree-lined boulevards, past tightly packed greystones and sidewalks full of stylishly dressed citizens.

The hotel was situated on a quiet side street not far from the river, and from the windows of Ed's room he could see the squarish towers of Notre Dame. The hunchback's haunt.

They met in the lobby and walked directly to the Cathedral, past cafes and souvenir shops selling French berets, t-shirts and plastic Eiffel towers.

"I'm sorry I said what I did," said Ed. "The priest revenge thing."

"Water off a duck's back," said CI Mullins. She waddled like a duck.

"One of my undercover personas was that of a bird watcher," said Ed. "And I can tell you, that is *not* how a duck walks."

They passed over the bridge to Notre Dame, along with dozens of tourists: couples, families and groups of Russians, Japanese, Chinese, German, British and American. The Seine river that passed under the bridge, around the small island where sat the Cathedral, was larger and the current more powerful than Ed had imagined. He watched as a tug maneuvered a flat barge upriver, around the turn.

Across an open plaza, the church rose before them like Godzilla rising from the sea. A beast of a building, spotted with gargoyles and long-necked fanged creatures like an infestation of worms and ticks and fleas. A nightmare of a church to an American tourist.

But inside, past the carved wooden doors, was a different story, a heavenly echo of a place, with its elegant arches, sky high ceiling and incredible stained glass windows diffusing unimaginable colors. Royal, heavenly colors of red and purple and bluish gray.

"My favorite church," said CI Mullins.

"But I thought you said ..."

"Still, my favorite church to visit," said CI Mullins as she went to one of the staff, flashed her badge, and asked in French about the Holy Crown.

The bearded man wasn't very friendly or helpful, but did point to the back of the Cathedral. They made their way around the center with its old wooden chairs, pews and huge pulpit. All the way to the back. In a kind of vestibule. A small sign in front of a red opaque container, roped off, announced the Crown. Inside the container they could just make out blurry shapes.

"The Crown of Thorns? Kept here?" Ed asked.

"I doubt it," CI Mullins said. "Most likely the Crown is kept in the church treasury. Or it's still out, getting restored."

They went to that side of the Cathedral, where the treasury was kept. She had a long conversation with a guard and then an official of the church. Returned to Ed.

"He confirmed the Crown was undergoing restoration," said CI Mullins. "But that it was no big deal. That it would be back in its case in time for tomorrow's public veneration."

"So we must wait for tomorrow?" said Ed. "He won't tell us where it's being restored?"

"He wouldn't give out that address," she said. "For security reasons. But tomorrow we can get a good look at the Crown and its thorns. See if any new ones have mysteriously grown back."

"How many thorns did it have before the restoration?"

"Barely any, I would think," she said. "Having been plucked for a couple thousand years."

"So if it has more than a handful, what are we supposed to do?" said Ed. "Seize it as evidence?"

"I don't know," said CI Mullins. "I guess we cross that London Bridge when we come to it."

They went outside the Cathedral, stepped back to admire the statues of Christ, of Mary, of the disciples and of the saints. Ed admired too the short curls that bounced round CI Mullins' face. As she talked excitedly about the history of the church, how it was old as sin, Ed noticed how her lips pursed when saying certain words.

"So what do we do with the rest of our day?" said Ed, leaning towards taking a nap back at the hotel.

"I suggest, first, a light lunch in the Latin Quarter," said CI Mullins. "Then this afternoon we visit the impressionist paintings at the Musee D'Orsay. The Gauguins, the van Goghs. Above all, the

Renoirs. Then, this evening, under the influence of impressionism and primitivism, under the sway of existentialism and nihilism, we get drunk on red wine in a dive I know on Rue Mouffetard."

"Funny," said Ed. "That's exactly what I was going to suggest."

She punched his arm. And it hurt.

"Careful," he told her. "Remember I'm an ol' man."

"You sure are," she said.

They walked together, to the bridge, watched the Seine flow below them. At the back of the Cathedral large trees blossomed. "When I die, I want to come back as a tree," she said.

"That might explain why I've always wanted to come back as a dog," he said. It took her a moment to get the joke. Then she hit him. Again.

14 The master restorer

They were an elderly couple, Johan and Edith. He, a master restorer, jeweler and antique shop owner in the sixth *arrondisement* of Paris, she the shop manager and biggest gossip on the street. Johan had long silver hair and black glasses whose thick lenses gave Johan the look of a frog with bulging eyes. Edith, younger, wore her long black hair in a bun and had the eyes of a pigeon, dull and always hungry. They made for a good couple, a good match that Edith's mother had arranged forty-three years before.

Johan was a master restorer, of all types of antiques: watches, furniture, and especially religious relics. He usually discussed each restoration with Edith, no matter how complex, to the point of boring her, but this time was different. This time he kept in the back room, with the door locked and asked her not to disturb him. Men came to confer with him on the project, at different times, a pair of clean-shaven Frenchmen, then, another time, a very different pair, two bearded Turks. Edith did not like the looks of either pair of men her husband was dealing with on this project and she told him so. She always told him so

"It's all right," he told her. "Sometimes the devil does good work."

"Be careful," she told him, reaching out with her spindly arm. "We've much to lose."

"But also much to gain," he assured her.

Two days before the once-a-month veneration of the Holy Crown held at the Cathedral of Notre Dame, Johan worked all night to be sure to finish this, his most challenging restoration.

A limousine pulled up around noon, stopping in the street before the shop, blocking traffic. The clean-shaven, nicely dressed Frenchmen entered, asking for Johan. Edith recognized these as the men who had first approached Johan about the project, men who looked less severe, less dangerous than the Turks. Edith watched as Johan handed to them an oversized briefcase. They checked the contents, out of sight of Edith. Satisfied, they departed, leaving Johan a BNP check that he waved in front of Edith's eyes.

"Let me put on my glasses," she said, then, "a good sum."

"A fine sum," said Johan.

"So that's that," said Edith, putting her glasses back in their case.

"Almost," said Johan. "There's a flip side to this one. For more. Much, much more. Please don't disturb anything in the back while I nap." He trudged upstairs and fell fast asleep on the same bed they had shared for so many years. The sleep of a man who was sure to pull off the swindle of a lifetime.

A few hours later, during a most pleasant afternoon, when the Mexican woman came in accompanied by her husband, her nanny and her baby, a beautiful Mexican woman whose sparkling eyes were captivated by the 1930s hat in the shop window, Edith attended to them while Johan continued to snore in the big bed, oblivious to the fact that his dear wife was about to lose him twenty million dollars.

15 An antique shop and a silly hat

In row twenty of American Airlines flight 48, Fernanda turned to Randy and said, "Why Paris?"

"What do you mean?" said Randy. "Are you asking me why I chose the most beautiful city in the world for our second honeymoon?"

"*Sí*," she said.

"Maybe because it's the most beautiful city?"

"She lives there, doesn't she?"

"Who?"

"You know. *Esa mujer*. Julie. Your ex-girlfriend. Who just happened to show up in Varanasi the same week as us. And you know what happened after that."

"She came for the Festival of Colors," said Randy. "A coincidence. And she was never my girlfriend."

"So you tell me," said Fernanda. "She still lives in Paris, yes?"

"To be honest, I don't know."

Fernanda waited for him to say, And I don't care. But he didn't. Instead he put his hand on hers. "Paris is incredible. You'll see. You'll end up loving it as much as me."

Constance wanted to leave for Notre Dame the moment they arrived at their hotel in the heart of Paris. To see the Crown of Thorns. "We can walk there from here," she said, but Randy said no.

"I do like the idea of a good walk though. We need to get the blood flowing after all that sitting. The best place for a walk is the Jardin de Luxembourg," he said. "A perfect place to stroll with the baby. Beds of flowers and columns of manicured trees. Lots of fountains and statues. Lawns where families picnic and lovers kiss."

"Did you ever?" said Fernanda. "Kiss her? Kiss Julie?"

"Course not," said Randy. "Why are you suddenly so jealous? I told you we were only friends. And that was years ago. When I lived in Paris. Before we married."

Fernanda gave him a long look. "I'm sorry. I love you so much, Randy. So much that sometimes it hurts, inside."

Silence. The only sound in the room was the baby cooing.

"Constance," Fernanda said, "tomorrow we are going to attend the Holy Crown veneration at Notre Dame, right?"

"Yes," said Constance. "Tomorrow."

"So let's wait until then to visit the Cathedral."

"OK," said Constance. She finished packing a diaper bag for little Rocky.

Randy walked over to the baby and pushed in her pudgy cheeks. "She was so nice on the flight," he said.

"I gave her a pinch of a herb that Paro sent me," said Fernanda. "A calming herb."

"Isn't that dangerous?" said Randy, concerned.

"All natural," said Fernanda.

"Still ..."

They left the hotel and walked the wide busy Boulevard Saint Michel.

"Did you notice?" asked Randy. "Those two men following us?"

"My guardian angels from Arkansas?" asked Fernanda.

Constance stole a look back. In the shuffle of well-dressed Parisians and more casually dressed tourists, the two men in black suits stood out. "That's them all right. Those FBI guys who watch you from the hill."

"I hope they enjoy this trip as much as we do," said Randy.

"At least we don't have to worry about being robbed," said Fernanda.

They entered the garden park gates next to a chateau, walked down steps to a wide pool encircled with flowers. Fernanda was surprised that the paths that ran through the park were gravel. "My good shoes are ruined."

"I told you to wear your tennis shoes," said Randy.

Constance, young and strong as a mule, easily carried the baby on her shoulder.

"Let me know if you want me to take her," said Fernanda.

Constance nodded.

The park was indeed special, the way the green trees were sculpted, like statues, and the bronze statues placed about the park were green as the trees. Like nature and art were blurring together, becoming one. Randy pointed this out to the girls. "The French love to arrange their gardens," he said.

They strolled past tourists and local Parisians, dodged joggers who kicked up dust ghosts, and walked through nets of shadows that flowed over their skin and their clothes. The Jardin de Luxembourg was a good place to share with all.

After walking the length of the park, and taking a long rest on metal chairs, warming themselves in the sun, Randy mentioned lunch. "I know a place that makes the best four cheese pizza in the world. Made with good stinky cheese as well as mozzarella."

They left the park and crossed over the busy street to Odeon Theatre with its Romanesque dome and wide columns.

They admired the building a moment, wondering how it must look inside, then Randy led them down a narrow street in cold shadow, a street populated with rows of the same cultured gray buildings they saw everywhere in Paris, buildings whose ground floors were book shops and curio shops and salons and tiny restaurants and expensive menswear and womenswear stores.

"Oh what a lovely hat," said Fernanda, stopping before the display window of an antique shop halfway down the block. The hat looked silly to Randy, a bit like Robin Hood's hat, pointed with a feather sticking out the back.

"Can we go inside?"

"*Vamos*," said Randy.

A cuckoo clock went off just as they entered the store full of old knicks-knacks and a grandma of a clerk behind the counter.

"*Bonjour Monsieur, Mesdames,*" she said.

"*Bonjour Madame,*" said Randy. "*Le chapeau. Combien?*" He pointed to the hat.

"This pretty thing, 100 Euros," said the French grandma, in heavily accented English, as she handed the hat into Fernanda's open hands.

"Around a hundred dollars," said Randy. He had to admit the hat looked good on Fernanda. Though of course, anything would look good on Fernanda.

"*Tres belle*," said the French grandma clerk.

"It's not too much, is it Randy?"

"No Fernanda. I think it's a good price."

He paid with his credit card.

"Do you have a box for the hat?" Fernanda asked.

"*Une boite pour le chapeau?*" asked Randy.

"*Une boite a chapeau?*" Grandma looked about. "Let me see." She disappeared into the back room, returned in a minute with a tall round hat box. The bottom of the box was stuffed with fresh tissue mixed with old newspaper.

"Perfect," said Randy. "*Parfait.*" Fernanda placed the hat atop the tissue inside, put the lid back on and slid the round box under her arm.

"Which way is Saint Michel Avenue?" he asked the grandma. "I think I may be turned around."

"You stay where?" she asked.

"At the Best Western. Near the Seine."

"Right and right. Saint Michel. Turn *a gauche*," said grandma, indicating each turn with a lean of her body and her hands. She waved goodbye to little Rocky who stirred in Constance's arms, opening her green eyes.

"*Merci Madame*," said Randy as they filed out.

"*Bonjour Monsieur. A bien tot.* See you soon."

Upstairs the master restorer woke with a start. Someone had stepped on his grave.

16 The hat box caper

"How could you!?" Johan yelled in French at poor Edith. "I take a nap and you give away our future?"

"It was a hat box. An empty box.," she insisted, flapping her arms like a frightened bird.

"Not empty," he said. "Hidden. I had hidden the most precious item inside. Beneath the tissue."

"You can get it back," she said. "They just left. A family. A stunning Mexican woman with her American husband and a nanny and their baby. Right and then right I told them. To Saint Michel. Then left to their Best Western Hotel. Not five minutes."

Johan dashed out the door, knocking off the counter in his mad rush a faux Marie Antoinette fan and a quill pen from the nineteenth century.

They were not in view, the Mexican woman and her entourage, so he turned right and then right at the corner, ran until his legs said no. He had to slow to a fast walk.

He reached Boulevard Saint Michel and turned left, still they were nowhere in sight.

He ignored the pain in his thighs and forced himself to rush to the corner of Saint Germain. He looked about to ask someone for directions to the Best Western Hotel, when he noticed in the picture windows of the first floor of Pizza del Arte a family that met Edith's description. Yes, there, on the floor, under their table, the hat box. On the floor! Twenty million dollars on the floor of a pizzeria!

He hobbled over, tried to calm himself. Told the server he wished to be by the window, by the door. He laughed inside as he sat within arm's length of the hat box, catching his breath.

He ordered red wine. Pretended to be looking at the menu as he spied on this family next to him. The Mexican woman was one of a kind. Such warm eyes. Even her voice was soothing. Simply tourists, he decided, as they talked about jetlag and so much to see.

Her husband looked distracted. The nanny was busy feeding the baby.

Johan decided to simply ask for the return of the hat box. That there had been a mistake. The box was not for sale. The words were almost out of his mouth when the Mexican woman asked the server directions to the bathroom. Upstairs, she was told. Her husband asked if the nanny wished to go. When she said no, he left the table with his wife, and together they climbed the winding stairwell.

Johan would have to wait.

The hat box sat practically abandoned. It called out to Johan. Take me! Take me!

Johan couldn't help himself. As soon as the nanny looked away, he scooped up the box and was out the door in a heartbeat. One block, two blocks, no one after him. He had done it. He, the master restorer, had restored their future!

He never saw what hit him. Only felt something slam him, and send him rolling. A car? No, he was on the sidewalk. He looked up and a hefty American in a black suit straddled him. No. Two men. They said nothing, absolutely nothing. Which was frightening. Yet worse, much worse, one of them grabbed the hat box. Johan spoke to them, called after them, tried to explain. But they ignored him. He could only watch, helpless, as they walked silently away, towards the restaurant. Johan painfully sat up, leaned against a storefront, straightened his glasses and wiped blood from a cut under his eye. He continued to watch as one of the strange Americans who had tackled him entered Pizza del Arte and stealthily returned the hat box back under the table in the exact spot it had been in before the attempted theft. Without the nanny noticing! And then the man left. Crossed the street with his partner. They stopped and stood casually on the opposite street corner, keeping an eye on the family in the restaurant like dark guardian angels. One of them lit a cigarette. Johan sat and watched them watch the Mexican woman come back down the stairs. Watched them watch her walk to her table and sit down. She said something to the nanny, who nodded. The husband returned as well, reached over and touched the baby. Their pizza arrived. They began to eat. As far as the family was concerned, nothing had happened.

What the hell?

17 Would you like a crepe with your Renoir?

Oblivious to the excitement of the hat box, FBI agent Ed Pushkin and Chief Inspector of the London Police Phoebe Mullins were just sitting down in the modern cave-like interior of Le Beau Crepe, in the Latin Quarter, a short stroll from the corner of Saint Michel and Saint Germain.

"Tell me about him," said Ed. "Your ex."

"No horrible death like your wife's, thank heavens," said Phoebe, taking up the tall thin plastic-coated menu covered with pictures showing crepes with Nutella, crepes with strawberries, crepes with ham and cheese. "We drifted. He cheated. So we called it quits."

"How old were you?"

"Being a woman, I'm not about to let that tidbit slip," said Phoebe. "Let's just say the marriage lasted about as long as an American made car."

"That short?" said Ed.

Phoebe smiled. She had been drawn to Ed moments after meeting him at the British Museum. Something about the way he carried himself, like a wounded bear. Her maternal instinct was to care for him, even though she could sense he had an edgy side, like something in him wanted out. Sometimes she felt that way too. She supposed everyone did, as they aged and sensed the Bloody Hound of Death closing on their tails.

"I've had lovers since," she told Ed, not noticing the waitress in her khaki-colored short dress.

"Good for you," said the waitress in accented English.

"Good for all of us," said Ed. He ordered a crepe with syrup only. Phoebe ordered a crepe with blueberries and a carafe of red wine for the two of them.

After lunch they started towards the D'Orsay Museum to see the impressionist paintings, only to be stopped by the enormous statue and fountain of Saint Michel. "So why a big fountain to a saint?" said Ed. "Why not a fountain to a national figure like Napoleon?"

"Saint Michael, as we know him in English, is an archangel, a warrior, celebrated by Christians, Jews and Muslims alike," said Phoebe. "He defeated his brother angel Satan, who rebelled against God."

"Muslims?" said Ed. "How do Muslims fit in this picture?"

"Oh, Muslims, being monotheists from the same Holy land as

Christians and Jews, share much of their religious lineage. Many of the same prophets. They're really brother religions. I suppose that's why they fight so much between themselves."

"I didn't know that," said Ed, following Phoebe as she pressed her way through the crowd of tourists and street performers in the plaza. They crossed to the Seine's riverwalk lined by magnificent old buildings, and walked upriver all the way to the museum.

Phoebe loved the Musee D'Orsay. She imagined herself one of the tall statues of black women in front, naked, strong and brave.

"I modeled for those statues," she told Ed.

"They don't do you justice."

She gave Ed her tour of personal favorites. First the ground floor to see Caillebotte's *Les raboteur's de parquet*, with its three shirtless men scraping the floor of a Paris apartment. Then they admired Courbet's The Source, where a naked woman's hips seem to fall out of the painting. And his *Femme nue au chien*, where a naked girl sits and plays with her poodle. Next came the panoramic paintings of the orient, like Belly's *Pelerin allant a La Mecque*, desert scenes that made you tired and thirsty.

Although she liked the art nouveau furniture on the second floor, Phoebe skipped that for now and took Ed up to the top to see the Impressionist paintings. Starting with the primitive Tahitian paintings of Paul Gauguin.

"He left his wife and family in France to paint in Tahiti, didn't he?" said Ed.

"To paint and have a lot of native sex," said Phoebe.

"Speaking of sex, why are all the women in these paintings naked?" said Ed.

"Because horny men like to paint us that way," said Phoebe.

"Makes sense."

"Still - you have to admit our bodies are so much more beautiful than men's bodies, with your chest hair and little elephant trunks down below."

"Or big elephant trunks," said Ed. "As the case may be."

She showed him Berthe Morisot's *Le Berceau*, where a mother is cooing to her baby in his cradle.

"You had no children?" said Ed.

"No," said Phoebe. "Mother and Inspector don't rhyme."

They moved on to a Renoir, where the woman's skin looked like lace.

"I feel like I want to rub my cheek against hers," said Ed. "Her skin looks so soft."

"Renoir is special," said Phoebe.

Van Gogh's hallucinogenic paintings, with their swirls, moved Ed. The pointillism paintings with all their dots less so.

Back on the street, along the river, Ed thanked Phoebe.

"I would never have gone by myself," said Ed.

"I'm glad I could show you," said Phoebe.

"I never thought the best thing I would see in Paris was a bunch of old paintings."

"Life is full of surprises," said Phoebe. "If you open up for them."

They decided to take a break at the hotel before dinner. Phoebe was tired, yet happy, after such a long walk with this interesting man.

"Thank you Ed, for coming with me to Paris. I know you think I am crazy, but I am sure we're on the right trail."

"Me too," he told her. "The trail of the missing thorn. Meet you in the lobby at six?"

"Sounds good."

They took the cramped elevator to their floor, face to face, up close. She could read the fatigue in his good eye. He wasn't young, but neither was she.

They went to their separate rooms. As her door closed, Phoebe wondered if one day she would share a hotel room with Ed. Share a hotel bed. Stranger things have happened, she supposed.

18 The evil eye

Constance was in heaven sitting at the table in the pizza place at the crossing of streets named after two of her favorite saints, eating thin fresh-made four cheese pizza and sipping Orangina from a squat nippled-glass bottle. A sudden flash as the door opened and an American family came in with two kids. The older child, a girl maybe twelve, hair in disarray, looked quickly away when Constance tried to get a smile. The little boy next to her stuck out his tongue. The waiter escorted the family to a table in the corner. Constance returned her attention to Fernanda.

"What are we going to do next?" she said.

"I think after lunch I will take a siesta," said Fernanda, wiping tomato sauce from her lips. "*Tengo sueno*." Wet spots over each nipple indicated her breasts were still producing, despite the tight wrap she wore under her blouse to discourage them.

"I'm not sleepy at all," said Randy. "Too excited about being here."

Fernanda felt a pain in her heart.

"I want to go see Notre Dame," said Constance. "Maybe even see the Crown."

"I can take the baby to the hotel with me," said Fernanda. "Leave you free. But you or Randy will have to carry my hat." She indicated the black box at her feet.

"I can," said Constance. "I don't mind." With the baby in one arm she reached for the hat box, but stopped when a chant from the corner table grabbed her attention.

"No, no, no. No, no, no, nooo!" The voice was childish, insistent. Grew louder. "No, No, No! No, No, No, Nooo!"

Was the strange American girl. Constance watched as she flung her menu onto the floor and started bouncing her head in time to the rhythm of her words, striking her palms on the table top with each NO, NO, NO!

The mother leaned over, spoke to her in an even voice, and was completely ignored. The father looked to the door, contemplating a getaway.

"NO, NO, NO, Nooo!" the girl screamed. The mother pressed on the child's arms, tried to stop her from banging. Her whole body bounced now. She was possessed.

The evil eye. Constance's neighbor back on the border had a boy like that. One day the boy, similarly possessed, went around smashing every window in their house with his head. When evil eye took you over, when it wound you up, there was no stopping it. Only a priest, speaking the ancient tongue, could halt such an attack.

The waiters came over, stood ready. But what could they do? All the diners stopped eating. All watched the drama, wanted to help. But what could they do? They all knew she was helpless, but also that they were helpless to help her.

"NO, NO, NO, Nooo!" The girl pleaded to some unseen spirit, banging with all her might. She jerked her head up, flashed crazy tear-filled eyes at them. At the whole room. Flashed the look of one drowning, of one mute, of one beating oneself to death.

"NO, NO, Nooo!"

There was no help for her here. Constance knew that. Wherever she was, in her agony, she could not be reached. Could not be pulled to safety.

Out of the corner of Constance's eye a figure passed. A handsome, calm woman with long black hair. She walked slowly towards the hysterical girl at the corner table. Was it? Could it be? Fernanda?

"NO, NO, Nooo!" the girl cried, slamming her fists down. Fernanda leaned over and wrapped the child in her arms. "No, no, Nooo," the girl said, struggling. Fernanda held tight, tears running down her own face. She lay her head against the girl's and whispered something. Something no one but the girl could hear. "No," the girl said, but already the fight in her was leaving, the devil retreating. Fernanda kissed the top of the girl's head, and released her. Constance stared. Waited. Waited for the devil to return. Waited in silence for what seemed like forever. But the possession was over. The girl sat quiet, the glitter of tear streaks on her cheeks like rainbows after a storm. She even smiled at Fernanda. Fernanda, who steadied her shaking self with one hand on the table.

The waiters traded amazed looks. The diners shook their heads. One even clapped. The father of the girl sat with his mouth open, apparently unable to move, while the mother rushed to embrace not her poor daughter but Fernanda.

"Thank you, thank you," the mother said.

"*De nada*," said Fernanda. "It's OK."

"Who are you?" the mother asked.

"She is Fernanda the Innocent," Constance said, running, with baby Rocky, to her side. "You have all just witnessed the first miracle of Fernanda the Innocent."

19 Separate paths

"Miracle indeed," mumbled Randy, as Fernanda stood talking with the mother of the previously distraught girl, handing out advice on natural calming herbs that might help in the future.

"Herbs from the Amazon," he heard her say. He paid the check, waited for Fernanda to finish with the family. She so liked to go on, at times. Especially about things that interested her, like herbs and witchcraft. OK, she didn't call it witchcraft, she called it natural healing. But one and the same, as far as Randy was concerned. Why she wanted to become a Peruvian shaman was beyond him.

And this so-called miracle - why, he had seen her do the same thing a hundred times. Babies (and he guessed the mind of this girl was like a baby's) just naturally calmed in her presence. As if they could sense the love she had for them. The love she had for all.

They left then: Randy, Fernanda with the baby, and Constance, each in their own direction, as agreed upon.

Fernanda carried the baby back to the hotel, a few easy blocks away, while Constance carried the hat box with her across the bridge, over the Seine river, to the courtyard in front of the Cathedral of Notre Dame.

Randy set off along the river a bit, then found himself crossing another bridge, farther down, into the Marais neighborhood of Paris. Originally a swamp, the Marais was now a diverse, cool part of the city, full of young couples, singles, gay folk, and Jews with their funny hats, and coats and curls. And Julie lived there, Julie the professional, Julie the romantic, Julie his ex-lover. He wondered if he could still find her place. Wondered if her door code had changed. Before he realized it, he was standing in front of her apartment building, his fingers testing the code he still remembered. The front door to the building clicked open in response to his fingers. He still had the touch.

Constance, meanwhile, had walked across the courtyard, then across the street to a brasserie on the corner, under the demonic gargoyle heads extending from the side of Notre Dame. Decorative rain spouts, that's all they were. Though the decorator should be shot. She took an outside seat, placing the black hat box in the other seat at the tiny round table, and ordered a glass of boiling water.

"C'est tout?" the waiter asked with surprise, straightening the vest of his shortened tuxedo-like outfit. "Are you sure, Mademoiselle? I will have to charge you as if for a drink."

"Yes," she said. "Very hot water, please."

He brought the glass and set it on the table where it steamed nicely, making the glass sweat. Constance waited for the waiter to retreat inside, then she reached in her pants pocket and pulled out a clear plastic sandwich bag containing a handful of Fernanda's ayahuasca herb. This was the herb Fernanda swore would allow one to speak to the spirits. The herb Constance had stolen from the quantities of herbs spread on the bed the day before they left. Constance intended to put the herb to good use. She intended to ingest the herb and enter Notre Dame Cathedral under the influence. Not so she could speak with Mary or Christ, no, she knew she would never be worthy of speaking directly with them. But perhaps the herb would allow her to speak with a saint? A saint who happened to be in the vicinity. Surely there must be saints galore inside a Cathedral as old and glorious and holy as Notre Dame. This was her hope anyway as she poured the herb into the hot water. She stirred the mix with a spoon, watched the plant diffuse. Ignoring the foot traffic, the voices and the occasional horn honk, she concentrated on the glass. She waited as the tea strengthened, wanting to be sure to consume a good dose.

It smelled bad. The smell alone made her stomach turn. She blew on the drink, sipped it. Tasted worse than it smelled. She decided to down it all, and did so, scalding her tongue. She coughed, put down a five euro bill. She got up and walked across the street, around the corner, remembering suddenly she had forgotten

Fernanda's hat! She ran back, the hat box was still there. She picked it up and returned to the front of Notre Dame. She got in line with the other tourists, only she knew she was no ordinary tourist. She was an emissary of the Church, a representative of Fernanda the Innocent. She stepped inside and was directed to a cloakroom to leave the hat box.

"Be careful," she told the man, "this box contains a hat belonging to Fernanda the Innocent."

"*Bien sure*," said the man as he handed her a piece of paper with a number to match the one he had placed on the hat box. "I will take absolute care for innocent Fernanda."

She walked then under the vaulted ceiling that arched to heaven, walked in that stone palace of God's that was one thousand years old. Almost as old as Christ himself. She couldn't help but rotate in the rays of colored light from the stained glass windows high above. She could practically smell the bluish gray, the rose red, the royal purple, no wait that smell was the smoke from small round candles burning under the windows. An old smell, of smoky prayers to God, smoke that rose up to the stained glass designs, intricate designs, more suggestion than form. More hallucination, than, ... wait. She had to sit down. Felt dizzy and her stomach rumbled. The herb. Taking effect. She made it to one of the wooden seats, in the back, away from the others. Put a hand to her chest. Her heart raced. Her breathing came labored. She lowered her face, didn't want anyone to notice how sick she felt. She lowered her head even more, couldn't help but do so, her head was so heavy, her eyelids of lead. Then, as she sat staring at the concave floor, her body quivering like a landed fish, it happened. Just as Fernanda had predicted. Just as Constance sorely wished. A saint appeared before her.

20 A coincidence

Loud long ring. Another. The room phone. "Damn," said Ed, stretching from his bed to the end table, picking up the receiver. He checked his watch. Almost 6 p.m.

"Hello?"

"Ed?"

Ed recognized the sound of his boss' voice, his FBI boss, not the interim one at INTERPOL. "Yeah, yeah, its me."

"Why didn't you answer your cell?"

"Because you didn't call," said Ed.

"I've been calling every five minutes since I got your email."

Ed fumbled with his cell. The room was just light enough, from the imperfectly curtained window, to allow him to see that the ringer was off. "Ringer was off, boss. It's on now."

"Great," and Ed could hear the sarcasm in his boss' voice.

"Now explain to me again what the hell you're doing on the other side of the English Channel?"

"Met a woman," said Ed.

"No doubt," said his boss. "I hope she's rich cause I'm not paying for that hotel."

"Seriously boss," said Ed. "I'm following a hot lead on the Holy Thorn case. We ... I mean I, think this might tie back to a restoration of the Holy Crown. The crown the stolen thorns came from originally."

"Let me get this straight," said his boss. "You think someone high in the Catholic organization is stealing thorns to reattach to the crown? Why wouldn't they just buy them?"

"Couple reasons," said Ed. "Number one, it's a sin to buy or sell for a profit relics of the first order. Number two, no one who had such a thorn would ever sell it, anyway. For any price."

"So you're going to arrest the Pope? I thought he lived in Rome. At some little place called, what, the Vatican?" The sarcasm was hot and heavy now.

"Not going to arrest anyone," said Ed, sitting up. "Not yet. The fully restored crown is being shown to the public tomorrow. Veneration they call it, at Notre Dame. I'll attend. Inspect the crown, inspect its thorns. Take pictures. Father Matthew of the Saint Anthony Parish told me he could recognize his thorn."

"Sounds farfetched Ed. Everything you've said sounds looney tunes."

"We gotta follow our hearts," said Ed. That got a laugh. "Don't worry about my expenses. I'll cover the cost of the hotel if this leads nowhere."

"Oh those INTERPOL fools will cover any expense. Just don't tell them you suspected the Pope. We don't need that in the media."

"Right-o." said Ed.

"OK now admit the real reason you're in Paris."

"What?" Ed scratched his chin. He should shave again before going out with CI Mullins.

"You heard she's there, in Paris, didn't you?"

"Who?" said Ed.

"Don't bother playing cagey with me."

"No really, who?"

"Your old Peru tail. Fernanda the Ripper."

That got Ed thinking. Remembering. Some good, some bad. "Curious."

"What?"

"I said that that is a curious coincidence," said Ed. "Her being here."

"Did she follow you or did you follow her?"

"Neither, as far as I know," said Ed. "Don't you have two guys tracking her? What do they say?"

"Second honeymoon, supposedly. Her and hubby. And the nanny and the baby."

"Some honeymoon," said Ed.

"Yeah. Today our boys stopped a guy from stealing a hat our Ripper had just bought at an antique and restoration shop."

Something clicked in Ed's gearbox of a brain. Wasn't a good click. More like something broke. Made the hair on the back of his neck crawl like spiders. Could there be a connection between Fernanda the Ripper and the theft of the thorns? Surely not, he told himself. Surely she isn't involved in this case.

"I assure you it's all a coincidence," he told his boss, "them being here the same time as me." But he told himself this was a new lead he'd have to follow up.

"OK, then. Enjoy Paris. Or Moscow. Or wherever the hell you're going to be tomorrow."

"Cheerio, boss." He hung up. Dragged himself out of bed. Felt more tired than before his nap. But CI Mullins wanted to dine, so he jumped into the narrow shower and took a mostly cold water rinse, given that the hot water only showed up for a few seconds at a time to scald him. By the end of the shower he was humming, a sure sign that despite everything, and mostly thanks to Mullins, he was enjoying this little jaunt.

21 Babies are like snapping turtles

Fernanda lay her angel on the bed, admired the handsome mouth that pursed, the eyelids that pressed together expressing distress. She knew the signs of the approaching bellow of hunger. She opened her own blouse and removed the stretch wrap that flattened her breasts. Ahhhh. Once released, her large milk-filled breasts hung heavily, like ripe fruit from the tree. She'd breastfeed the baby one last time.

She sat next to little Rocky, lifted the squirming child, and offered the cutie her left nipple. Rocky pounced. Aiee! Every time Fernanda was surprised at how tightly, and how painfully for her, the baby could clinch her gums, pinching the nipple. Like a snapping turtle.

As the little one fed, making those slurping sounds she always did, Fernanda stared out the window. She could see the top half of the twin towers of Notre Dame. She appreciated the beauty and history of this city, but still had doubts why Randy chose this place for their second honeymoon.

She remembered the Frenchwoman, Julie, who she'd met in

India during that project with Randy, remembered how elegant she was, how sophisticated. Julie wore makeup and did her hair, whereas Fernanda wore none and merely brushed hers. Fernanda was a natural beauty. Julie, on the other hand, was a styled beauty, a woman who tweaked what beauty she had to make her irresistible to men like Randy. Fernanda knew and feared this. That Julie could be irresistible to Randy.

She shifted the baby around to the other breast. Winced again as Rocky latched onto her.

"Enjoy while you can, little turtle," she told Rocky. "Next time it's the bottle for you."

22 Goodbyes hurt

Finding himself in front of Julie's apartment building, as if transported there by magic, Randy entered and made his way up the circular stairs that wrapped around the iron-laced elevator shaft like an anaconda wrapped around a tree.

He knocked at her door. Heard someone rustling inside, checking the peephole. It opened.

She was more beautiful than he remembered. How long had it been?

"Julie."

She dodged his embrace, moving like a ghost in her white wispy nightgown. Still, she let him inside.

He looked about, remembering as he did so the unique personality of her furnishings: the paper-thin silk tapestries on the wall stenciled with exotic oriental figures, the bookshelves full of poetry and ancient history. The low leather couch fronted by a misshapen gnarly coffee table, a whimsical chair in the corner.

He turned to her, saw the question in her amber eyes, which sparkled with soft Paris light entering the bay window overlooking a garden of trimmed bushes and birdless trees.

"Why?" she asked.

"I didn't think you would be home," he said.

"You came hoping I wouldn't be home?" she said. "That sounds like you." She turned from him. Touched the wall. "I had a premonition. This morning. That I must not leave for work. So here I am."

She turned back to him. Her eyes shiny.

"I think, more than anything, I've missed those eyes," Randy told her.

She smiled, a sad smile, walked the narrow hall to her kitchen. He followed, feeling the intimacy of the situation the deeper he went inside her apartment.

The kitchen was a typically cramped Parisian one, all white, with a two burner stove, a sink, cabinets and a small table for two. Randy admired the sheen of Julie's limp hair as she bowed her head, looking for something in a drawer. She appeared to Randy like something out of a medieval drawing he'd seen - of a woman with bowed head, praying. She was almost holy. Someone to revere.

She moved to the table and sat down. An airy lightness about her movements. He sat across from her. "I think I came to give you a proper goodbye," Randy said. "In India, I didn't get the chance."

She drew a long silver knife onto the table top before her. "My eyes, you said?"

He looked from the knife to her face, which looked paler now, fragile as Murano glass. "Yes, I've always loved your eyes."

"Then have them," she told him, "you've already got my heart." She raised the knife, sharp end pointed towards her face, and lowered her eyes towards the blade.

"No!" Randy cried, leaping across the table, grabbing her arm. The knife clanged to the floor as they struggled. He gripped her tight as he moved round to take her entirely into his arms. He held her then, till he felt her go limp. Heard her begin to cry.

"I loved you," she told him, between sobs. "I loved you so much, it still hurts every day."

"I loved you too," he said, feeling her body shake against his chest. A poor quivering thing. A thing to be protected. "I love you still."

Once she'd calmed, he suggested they go outside, take a walk to the canal. He waited in the living-room as she changed, then followed her down the plushly carpeted wooden stairway, to the exit. She pushed a button on the wall that released the building lock with a click, and he opened the heavy door for her.

Was marvelous to be walking next to Julie, in Paris again, even if she would not take his hand. Reminded him of those days when they first met, three years ago. Reminded him too of their time together, more recently, in India. Before the near disaster.

As they walked along Randy could feel the spirits of all the Parisian lovers that had walked that sidewalk before them, the last thousand years, now crowding around them, cheering them on. On to what, though? To cheating on his wife? His step slowed.

"What's wrong," Julie asked. "Did you forget something?"

"No," said Randy. "I remembered something."

"We're just taking a walk," she told him. "Nothing wrong in that."

"No," he agreed. "Nothing wrong. Only ..."

"I know," she said. "Fernanda. But let's not think on that now. I just want to enjoy your company. I've missed you."

They walked past an antique bookshop with books propped open showing imaginary maps of the world, in a street lined with charming buildings from another age.

"Almost every day I remember a certain way you looked, or words you said, that moved me," he told her.

"Only almost every day?" she said, and she took his hand, causing him to catch his breath.

They reached the wide basin with its small anchored boats. Beyond the basin ran the Canal Saint-Martin with its multi-level locks, its promise of quiet, slow adventure.

"I love ..." he started to say, but she said, "No. Don't say that word. We can't say that word anymore. Too dangerous."

"OK, I won't say it anymore." He felt joyful being so near her. Light headed. Jet lag, he told himself. I am vulnerable. But he didn't care, he let himself be whatever he would be. Surely Life knew what it was doing, allowing them time together here alone.

They fell into a kind of meandering dance around the canal walk, moving apart, then close together again, yelling to each other, then whispering in each other's ears.

"I don't love you," she told him.

"You're not to say that word," he told her.

"I know," she said, "that's why I said the opposite."

"You didn't say the opposite. You said you don't love me."

"I do," she said.

"You do what?"

"Don't love you."

"OK," he said.

"I don't love you," she said, frowning, pushing him away. "I adore you!" And she threw herself in his arms.

He felt her body quiver. Held her tighter. Wished they could stay like that forever, a new monument along the canal, for all the boatmen and all the strollers to see. What a fool he was. What had he done? This was not Goodbye at all. This felt more like Hello.

23 Constance has a vision

Her surroundings fell away and Constance found herself no longer in the great Cathedral but kneeling on a cliff edge overlooking a waterfall. A waterfall coming from her insides. She leaned closer and realized the rush of falling liquid wasn't water at all, but stars, innumerable stars, bright white, fading yellow, gold and silver stars, all tumbling into an abyss. They fell silently. Her fingernails sparkled with the brilliance of their passing.

"Where am I?" she asked the saint before her, a whiff of a girl, a beauty, in a white Roman robe.

"Here," replied the saint.

"But where is here?"

"How could I tell you, so you could understand?" The saint said, stepping closer to Constance. "You are at the end. You are at the beginning. You are somewhere in between. You are here."

"I know you, don't I?" said Constance.

"You know all us saints by heart," said the figure. "Remember the story of Eulalia? I am Eulalia, though I would prefer that you call me Lula."

"Eulalia?" said Constance. This was incredible. To be talking to a saint! "Yes, I remember. You were only twelve when you refused to make an offering of salt to the pagan gods. The emperor had you tortured and killed."

The saint nodded.

"Tell me Eulalia," Constance started.

"Lula, please."

"Tell me Lula, tell me how I can help my cousin Fernanda, Fernanda the Innocent, to reach her potential," said Constance. "Tell me, she is the next Messiah, isn't she?'

"Perhaps," said Lula. "Does she want to be?"

"What does it matter what she wants?"

"You want her to be."

"Yes. Of course. We're in such need of another Messiah."

"We?"

"The Church," said Constance. "And the world. The entire world is in such need. Tell me Lula, how can I convince her?"

"Life will show the way."

Constance's body rolled forward, headfirst, out of her seat, onto the hard stone floor. The pain from the blow on her forehead returned her to her senses. She opened her eyes, surprised to find herself back in the Cathedral of Notre Dame. Scrambled to her feet before anyone noticed. Her hands were sticky from something on the floor. She wiped them on her pants, wiped her mouth too, and headed to the exit.

At the cloakroom she handed the man her ticket. He brought Fernanda's hat box, saying, "I took extra special care. Such a special hat for innocent Fernanda." He gave Constance a wink.

Constance gave him a questioning look.

He winked again.

What was he trying to tell her?

Constance hurried out the door. She no longer felt sick, only confused by her talk with the saint, and the strange winking of the doorman. What had she learned, really, from the saint's visitation? Frustrated, she sat on a garden ledge in front of the church to think. A group of tourists stampeded by, knocking over the hat box.

The top came off the rolling box, and the hat slid out, onto the ground. And something else poked out of the hatbox. Something round and light brown. Curious, Constance picked up the box, reached in past the hat and pulled out the round thing half hidden in the packing.

She brought it up before her eyes, and felt her heart skip two beats. How was this possible? How was this possible?

In her hand she held nothing less than the *Holy Crown of Thorns!*

The Crown of Jesus, the Crown of the first Messiah!

She pricked a finger on one of the thorns as she turned it in her hands. She gasped as a drop of her blood appeared, just as His blood must have appeared two thousand years ago.

She remembered then the words of Saint Lula, that Life would show the way. She realized then that the winking cloakroom attendant must have been some kind of Angel working for Lula. An Angel who had removed somehow the Crown from its place in Notre Dame, and placed it in her hat box. For Fernanda. Given to Constance to give to Fernanda. Obviously she, Constance, was meant to crown Fernanda the Innocent as the new Messiah, the one who would unify the Church and all the peoples of the world. To bring about the End Times.

"Oh how wonderful," a tall woman said, disturbing Constance from her reverie. "Where can I buy one?"

"*Lo siento,*" Constance told her, "one of a kind." She placed the Crown back in the box with Fernanda's hat. She put the lid on the box, stood, and made her way through the tourists, over the white gravel of the plaza, to the bridge over the River Seine.

She glanced at the brown current churning away. Felt one with it. For it was headed in the right direction, as was she. Downriver. Downriver to her destiny. By taking the herb ayahuasca while visiting Notre Dame, home to the Holy Crown, Constance had confirmed her suspicion that she was and would forever be the first disciple of the final Messiah.

24 A small chance

Constance returned to the hotel and hid the Crown in her room before visiting Fernanda and the baby in theirs. The room smelled of breast milk and a dirty diaper. Fernanda was on the phone. She motioned for Constance to sit next to her. She tilted the handset so Constance could hear as well.

"So they stopped coming?" Fernanda repeated into the phone. Her breath smelled of red wine.

"Word must have got out," said the tinny voice. "That you'd gone. The ones already here begged me to tell where you went, but I wasn't about to betray my dear Fernanda."

"Thank you, Chance," said Fernanda. "I'm sure this frenzy will go away. If only I hadn't agreed to that interview."

"It's the world wide web," said Chance. "It takes kittens and turns them into monsters."

"Like me?"

"No, I mean, a rumor that would take years to reach a million people spreads now in a day or two. It's a whole new world. Of rumor and instant stardom. But we did make a pretty penny on mine fees, thanks to your notoriety. So hurry back."

Fernanda laughed just as the door opened and Randy came in, looking flushed.

"Randy," said Fernanda. He looked at Fernanda, gave a weak smile. Fernanda's face fell. Even Constance could tell, after weeks of seeing them interact back in Arkansas, that something was amiss.

"What about Randy?" asked Chance on the phone.

Fernanda started to say something, then got up, handing the phone to Constance. Constance watched as she went to the bathroom and closed the door. Randy's head went down.

"Anyone there?" asked the phone.

"One second," said Constance. She passed the phone to Randy, picked up the baby and went to her own room. Something's not right between them, she thought. But what did that matter? All that mattered was that Fernanda was the Messiah and she, Constance, was her disciple. Laying the baby down carefully on the bed in her room, Constance sat at the tiny desk by the window overlooking Notre Dame, opened her computer and began to blog to the world about the miracle at the Paris restaurant today. How Fernanda the Innocent chased the devil from a child with a single word. She decided to keep secret for now, from her readers on the internet, about how a saint had given her the Holy Crown, as she wanted that to be a grand surprise.

25 An evening, a lifetime

"So what do you think we will find tomorrow?" asked Ed as CI Mullins ate her chocolate mousse. The meal had been decent, steak for him and flounder for her, though at the inflated prices of Paris he couldn't help but feel cheated.

"A thorn or two, here's hoping," she said. "Otherwise, the trip was for bloody naught." She licked the spoon. Not at all in an erotic way but it sure struck Ed as erotic. Made him want to bite her neck.

She motioned to the waiter and insisted on paying the check.

"But I can expense the meal," said Ed.

"Doesn't matter," she said. "It's my treat and that is that."

"Trick or treat?" said Ed, feeling the wine in his legs as he stood. So she paid and they went outside into the Paris night.

"By the way, I like your Halloween outfit," he told her.

"What? Oh, you're making a drunken joke," said CI Mullins. "I'd better drive tonight."

And she steered him on the sidewalk a few steps.

"Seriously," he said, moving alongside her, almost reaching for her hand. "I do like your outfit." She had on tight jeans, a gray tank top, multicolored tennis shoes, and for earrings two orange plastic discs. Her hair, in tight curls, bounced when she stepped, her orange lipstick glistened when she spoke. "Only," he said, "I worry you'll be cold."

"We'll warm up walking," she said, speeding up.

They headed down Saint Michel, away from the river area with its ton of tourists, to the retail district, with its clothing shops and luggage shops, pharmacies, hotels and movie theaters.

They said little, walking briskly. She began to hum.

"Are you humming?" he asked.

"No," she said, and stopped humming.

"I do that sometimes," he said, as they continued walking.

"What?"

"Hum when I'm happy."

"I'm not so happy," she said, "that I would actually hum about it."

"Oh," he said.

She began to hum again, letting her hand slap lightly against his as they walked.

They passed Place de la Sorbonne, with its gray paving stones, and continued down to Rue Soufflot, where they turned left. He could see a large lighted dome ahead.

"The Pantheon," she told him. They strolled slowly around the building.

"Looks sealed up," he told her. "Uninviting. Like a tomb."

"It was originally built as a church to house the holy relics of Saint Genevieve, the patron saint of Paris," said CI Mullins.

"What is her story?" Ed said.

"Pretty amazing," said CI Mullins. "Around the year 400, she talked God into persuading Attila the Hun not to invade Paris."

"Is that all?" said Ed.

"After she died, her relics continued to perform miracles."

"What are her relics? What's left of her from the year 400?"

"Well, nothing actually. What remained of her was burned during the French Revolution. 1790s. And the Pantheon was changed to house important French statesmen instead."

"So a tomb," said Ed. "But not for her anymore."

"It is, still, that, sort of," said CI Mullins.

"Nothing is simple," said Ed.

The street funneled at the backside of the Pantheon into Rue de l'Estrapade, which ended at a small circle with a fountain called Place de la Contrescarpe. They hung a right and started down a steep cobblestone street called Rue Mouffetard. Largely pedestrian, as couples roamed the sidewalks and the street.

"Look out!" said CI Mullins, pushing Ed aside just as a shop woman tossed a bucket of water with shredded lettuce and carrot shavings into the gutter.

"You're hit," said Ed.

"Just a flesh wound," said CI Mullins, knocking a carrot shaving from her wet pants leg. "I've had worse."

The shops were closing up, while the restaurants and bars, with their faded red canopies, were filling. CI Mullins directed Ed to her favorite place, a bar with a darkly wooded interior, with hatchets and maces on the walls, and a rough-looking local crowd.

"Ah," said Ed. "Attila the Hun's birthplace."

They sat at a candle-lit table made of heavy swamp wood, and began their night drinking absinthe, invented by the gods to make men first happy, then drive them mad.

Ed returned from the bathroom, maneuvering unsteadily back to their table. God knew what time it was. He sat down heavily. Fell back into their conversation.

"How is it you know Paris so well, CI?"

"You can't call me Phoebe, can you? Just can't do it?" She refilled his glass from the carafe.

"I'm a bird watcher," said Ed. "In bird watching, you can't just call a bird any old name. You have to use their official name."

"You're drunk," said CI Mullins. "And you're no bird watcher."

"Undercover," said Ed. "That was my undercover story. My cover story."

"And what's your story now?"

"I don't want to hear my story," said Ed, downing half his glass. "I want to hear yours."

Laughter at another table caught their attention. A toast was being made. Every face at that table seemed to be glowing. Ed wondered if his face was aglow as well.

"After University, I moved to Paris," said CI Mullins. "I took classes at the Alliance Francaise. I studied philosophy and literature at the Sorbonne. I was young. I was looking for something."

"Did you find it?"

She hesitated, moved the glass in a circle on the table, searching for the answer herself.

"I found a young man. I found love. I found heartbreak. I left." She leaned towards him, crinkling her eyes with a sad smile. Another toast was announced at the nearby table, but neither of them looked away. They shared each other's gaze. Shared the tender moment, as their hearts slowed and in all the world there was only the two of them that mattered. Ed felt a warmth growing inside his chest, a warmth that had been missing a good long time. He reached over and gently placed his hands on Phoebe's.

26 The master restorer calls for reinforcements

"*Tu ne l'a pas obtenu?*" said the master restorer's wife Edith. "You didn't get it?"

"You didn't tell me they had bodyguards!" yelled Johan, exaggerating his limp.

"Bodyguards?" said Edith, biting her nails. "She must be some kind of princess. Or a queen."

"Two gorillas. They almost killed me."

"What are you doing?" she asked as he picked up the phone.

"I have to let them know," said Johan.

"Who?"

"The ones that owe me still. They have the muscle in town to get it, not me."

"The Turks?" she asked.

He nodded.

"And they will still pay you?"

"If they get it, they will pay me. Millions." said Johan, dialing. "Surely, they must."

Edith went to the other side of the room, put her hands together and teeter-tottered, praying that God would help them in their hour of need, else Johan would always hold this against her. She caught snatches of her husband's conversation, "Mexican" and "Best Western, Latin Quarter" and "hat box." Lasted but a few minutes.

Hanging up, Johan turned and sighed. He walked slowly over to his long suffering wife. He put his arms around her, told her it would be alright. "They said to not fear, that they would handle it in the morning. "

Edith began to cry with relief.

27 A night confession and morning arrangements

"I had to go see her," said Randy to Fernanda's backside in the hotel bed. "I had to check on her hearing, after the incident in India."

"After all this time? You couldn't have called her? From home?"

"I tried. Julie wouldn't take my calls. Or couldn't hear the phone ring. That's why I went to see her today. In person."

"And?"

"She's OK."

"And us, Randy, how are we?" said Fernanda. "*Yo, me siento cansada, cansada.*"

"I feel tired too. The long flight." He knew what she meant, though. His meeting with Julie hadn't gone as planned. He had never intended to see her again, after today, and now all he could think was, when would he see her again?

Fernanda turned to face him. "Tell me Randy, *dime la verdad.* Have you had sex with that lady?"

"Of course not," Randy said, raising up. "I've told you many times now. She is an old colleague. I was concerned about her. She could've died in India."

In the dark Randy could just make out her questioning eyes. He touched her soft cheek. "I love *you*," he told her. She let him pull her close, embrace her. In a few moments they were undressing, under the covers, and making love.

"The baby is colicky," said Fernanda the next morning as Randy entered the room with fresh croissants and coffee for breakfast. "And Constance has decided, after all her talk, not to go to the veneration."

"So we're not going?" said Randy, sitting at the desk, taking a bite of croissant. Tasted wonderfully flaky. Melted in his mouth.

"You can still go," said Fernanda.

"Actually I was looking forward to it. I've never attended service in Notre Dame," said Randy. "They have a pipe organ. One of those huge ones. Why don't you come with me? We can leave colicky Rocky with Constance."

"You go," said Fernanda. "I want to rest today."

Randy hesitated. "I'll stay with you."

"No," she told him. "I want you to go and take pictures for

Constance and me."

"OK," said Randy, reluctantly. He was almost afraid to go alone today, afraid that he would find himself again at Julie's door. But he grabbed the camera and set out. "See you later. I'm off to venerate, whatever that is."

28 Ed and Phoebe, the morning after

Morning. Ed showered and dressed. And tried to remember if they had kissed goodnight, as he knocked on CI Mullins door.

"You're up early," CI Mullins said, giving him a peck on the lips.

Well there you go. There was your answer, Mister Ed. You dumb clod. You got so drunk last night you kissed a Chief Investigator of the Royal British Police. And now she is kissing you back, in broad daylight. Not drunk at all. You or her. Well, maybe a little drunk, still. Certainly hung over. That was potent poison last night. But this can't be good. Can it?

Probably not good. Probably not good at all.

"I'll be ready in a minute, come in."

He hesitated. God only knew what might happen if he found himself alone in her room with her. "I'll wait downstairs," he said. "I want to get some juice."

"Get some for me too," she said, and closed the door.

Thank goodness. For that door. He was obviously losing control of himself. Senile, most likely. Chasing a younger woman like Phoebe. Sure she has wrinkles but that don't mean much, age-wise. He wondered how old she was. Maybe she told him last night but last night was a blur.

When she came down, he was embarrassed how shabbily he was dressed compared to her: a black gown, red heels, diamond earrings and a red scarf.

"Trick or treat?" she asked him.

"Treat," he told her. "Definitely a treat. You look beautiful. I am honored."

She raised her eyebrows, surprised. "You must still be drunk," she told him. "Let's go." And she took his arm.

"What about your juice?"

"I'm plenty juiced up as it is," she said. "Today we solve a crime."

Early as it was, already a crowd, dressed in their Sunday best, formed a fat line to get into the Cathedral.

CI Mullins accompanied him to the front. Ed flashed his FBI badge.

"*Qu'est que c'est?*" asked the thin Frenchman, the first in line.

"INTERPOL," said CI Mullins.

The Frenchman grudgingly gave way to them.

Almost an hour passed before they were let in. Ed was ready to drop, but he advanced forward with the crowd, to the front of that magnificent palace of God that was ten times taller than any church Ed had ever entered. He and CI Mullins got a front row seat. Wooden seat. Hard wood. Ed began to worry, with his iffy back, that by the end of the veneration, instead of being cured of all his ills, he might be crippled.

After a while organ music washed down on them from heaven, as if played by the giant atop Jack's beanstalk. A procession of priests entered, in white robes, and wearing white gloves like his mom used to when she took him to church in the fifties. When he was still innocent. Before them paraded a robed man waving a bucket of smoking incense.

Ed noticed, as they proceeded towards the front, that the white robed priests carried on their shoulders, like pallbearers, an ornate container on a wooden stretcher. Reaching the priest's podium, they ceremoniously set the box down and removed from it, for display, a round clear tube decorated with gold filigree. Inside the tube he could just make out, what looked like, intertwined twigs.

"The Crown," he whispered to CI Mullins, who nodded, then

sneezed.

"God bless you," he said.

"God bless us all," said a heavyset American man who was seated, along with his wife, beside them. A choir began to sing behind the podium, behind the Crown.

Ed looked the large man next to him over, then whispered to him. "Do you know if that is sealed glass around the Crown?"

"A rock crystal container," the man said. "Here." He handed Ed a brochure all about the Crown, full of close-up pictures.

A white robed priest with special red markings on his chest and a red disk of a cap took the podium and gave a sermon in French. Meanwhile Ed reviewed the brochure. Took a good look at a close-up of the Crown, re-read all that it said about it. Took out his camera and zoomed in on the real Crown and its container. Shook his head at what he saw. Stuffed the brochure in his pocket, and closed his eyes. CI Mullins elbowed Ed several times during the sermon, to wake him.

Finally a change, the priest stopped talking and carried the Crown in its clear circular container nearer the congregation. More smoky incense was spread. CI Mullins sneezed again as the white robed priests formed a line, and one by one they took their turn in front of the Crown, kissing the crystal that surrounded it.

People from the crowd joined the line of veneration. CI Mullins jumped up and dragged Ed along as well. The line moved quickly. They found themselves before the Crown.

"INTERPOL," pronounced CI Mullins, taking the camera from Ed and snapping a close-up of the Crown before anyone could stop her. Then she noticed what Ed had noted from afar. The Crown of Thorns was naked. She couldn't spot a single thorn along its twisty body.

"Where are the thorns?" she asked, dumbfounded, looking to Ed who was, incredibly, leaning down to kiss the Crown.

She felt a jerk on her arm. One of the white robed priests had grabbed her. "We get that question a lot," said the priest, a serene smile breaking on his acned face as he guided her away from the Crown. "The thorns were plucked over the centuries. Given, by the various owners of the Crown, as little miracles themselves to venerate."

"But I heard the Crown was being restored," said CI Mullins.

"Restored every few years to keep from falling apart," said the priest, releasing her as Ed jogged up. "But surely you didn't think we would put back the thorns?"

"Of course not," said Ed for her. "Let's go now, Honey. You've had enough excitement for one day." He took her by the arm and led her outside.

"They didn't put back the thorns," said CI Mullins, still stunned.

"No," said Ed. "No thorns." He handed her the brochure. "Seems the Crown has been thornless now for over five hundred years."

"Then why, Ed? Why did someone steal the thorns?"

Ed escorted CI Mullins onto the open plaza before Notre Dame. He wished he could think of something to say to cheer her up, but their little adventure was over. No crime would be solved today. No big bust in Paris. Not by them anyway. "Maybe they stole the thorns for another Crown?" was all he could think to tell her.

"But it is one of a kind," said CI Mullins. She looked like she was about to cry.

"Yeah, I know," said Ed. He felt a strange vibration in his pocket. Remembered his cell. Pulled it out. "One sec," he told CI Mullins. He walked just far enough away to have some privacy, and answered. "Hey Boss."

"Thought you might want to know," said his boss. "Something's happening with your Peru tail."

"You mean Fernanda?"

"Yeah. The ripper."

"What's happening?"

"Not clear at this point. Maybe a kidnapping."

"She's kidnapped someone?" asked Ed, incredulous.

"No, maybe she is being kidnapped."

"Maybe? What does that mean?"

"There's more," said his boss.

"I'm listening," said Ed.

"Maybe you were right about the thorn trail leading to Paris."

Ed started to say, No, but caught his tongue. "Go on."

"You know we've been tailing her."

"With the Bobbsey Twins, yes."

"Well we also bugged her room, and placed a camera."

"Not surprised," said Ed.

"Well…" and his boss went on to explain all that had happened in Fernanda's hotel room while he and Phoebe were sitting in the church, breathing toxic incense. He noted down the address, and closed his phone. Walked back over to his favorite British cop and said, "I've got good news and bad news."

"The good news?"

"You were right. They did steal the thorns to put on the Crown."

"But we just saw …" said CI Mullins.

"We saw a knockoff, a fake," said Ed. "The real Crown, the one now replete with thorns, is here in Paris. Presently sitting on the head of one of the most beautiful women I know."

CI Mullins frowned. "OK. And the bad news?"

"This woman I know, the woman wearing the Crown," said Ed, rubbing his hands together, barely able to believe himself the crazy words he was coming out with, "this woman is possibly a serial killer."

CI Mullins took a moment to digest that news.

"Oh," she said finally. "Is that all?"

"No," said Ed, shaking his head. "The serial killer with our Crown is, at this very moment, being kidnapped from her hotel."

"Bloody hell."

29 A taste of Randy on Julie's lips

Julie was just about to leave for work when she heard a knock on her door.

"Who is it?"

"Me."

She opened the door to find Randy smiling sheepishly.

"I had to see you again," he said.

He stepped forward, and there, in the doorway, they came together, exchanging a kiss so laden with emotion, Julie thought she might faint. Instead she broke into laughter. They both did.

Randy turned then and ran, down the stairs, like a naughty boy getting away. Which felt right to Julie. After such a kiss you need distance for the reverberations to take their full affect.

I want him, she told herself. I want him more than ever. She thought about her predicament, realized there was only one thing to do.

She left her flat and instead of going straight to work she took the metro to Saint Michel. Only a few tourists mingled in the area as she walked to the Best Western hotel. The sky was rosy, the air a little cool. She dodged a double bus, with its peculiar accordion connection like one of those slinky wiener dog toys. A child's face appeared in a window of the second floor, a child who stared at her so intently she actually stopped, and double-checked how she looked in the store's picture window before her. She saw nothing amiss on the outside, but her eyes, she'd never seen her eyes look like that, as if her heart were about to burst right through them.

She hurried on to the hotel.

At the front desk she asked for Randy and Fernanda. The clerk picked up the receiver and rang the room.

30 The Crown finds its new owner

Constance barely slept the night before the veneration, as she had her own veneration planned in the morning with Fernanda and the Crown. Even little Rocky seemed overly excited, colicky, and not keen to drink from a bottle. Constance had already visited Fernanda once this morning, explaining that she did not plan to go to the veneration at Notre Dame. When she heard Randy bring breakfast, she hurried over with the baby in one hand and the diaper bag in the other. Snuggled in between the pampers was the Holy Crown.

She listened as Fernanda told Randy to go on alone. Go on, Constance told him silently as well, I have business with Fernanda the Innocent.

Randy did leave then, to attend the veneration. Constance finished eating two croissants with butter while she and Fernanda took turns rocking the little one. When baby Rocky fell asleep, Constance broached the subject of her own visit the day before to the grand cathedral. She dared not mention that she had ingested ayahuasca, that fact was better kept a secret. Instead she stuck to a simple telling.

"It is a most holy place," she started. "Ancient and inspired. I felt the weight of God's attention the moment I entered. So I prayed to him, prayed that he would give us guidance. That he would send us a sign to prove that you were the Chosen One. The next Messiah."

"But dear Constance, I am not ..."

"And He did," pronounced Constance, taking the Crown triumphantly out of the diaper bag. "He gave me this for you when I left."

"Who gave you that?"

"An Angel of God."

Fernanda leaned over to get a closer look. "What is it?"

"This was Christ's Crown," said Constance. "Now it is yours." She handed it out for her cousin to take.

Fernanda got up and backed away instead, her eyes wide. "Christ's Crown? The one they are going to venerate today?"

"The one they cannot venerate. For we have it."

"You stole the Crown of Thorns?"

"An Angel gave it to me, at Notre Dame, to give to you." Constance rose and placed the Crown gently on Fernanda's head. "This is the sign I asked of God. The sign that you *are* the Messiah."

Fernanda put her hands to her head, touching the Crown with her finger tips. Her expression changed, a pained look clouding her face. Constance could tell the truth was dawning on her, the inevitability of her destiny.

"I can feel Him," Fernanda said, sitting back down. "Through the Crown. I feel his suffering. Oh God. How he suffered."

"The innocent, the loving, they are the ones to suffer the most," said Constance.

Just then the phone rang.

31 Julie leads with her heart

A woman's soft voice on the other end of the line told Julie the room number. Asked her to come up.

She rode the tiny elevator, steeling her resolve as each floor dinged by. The elevator door opened. She pulled the metal cage to the side and exited. Walked the carpeted hall to the room, her feet silent, the whole world holding its breath, before the elevator door closed behind her.

The hotel door to Randy and Fernanda's room opened just before she knocked.

She recognized Fernanda - a brown natural beauty for sure - but what was that on her head? What a strange thing to be wearing. Looked like a small wreath but without the flowers. Only intertwined twigs with inch-long thorns – what kind of a headband was that?

"Hello," Julie said, reaching out her hand. "We met in India. A while back."

"I remember," said Fernanda. "My husband told me he visited

with you yesterday. To check on your health. Please sit down."

"No," said Julie, glancing at the nanny and the baby. She tried to calm herself, tried not to scream the next words. "I've come to tell you that I am in love with your husband. And that he is in love with me." She was screaming the words inside. I love him! I love him!

Fernanda stepped back, grimacing, her big brown eyes sad. Her mouth opened as if she had been punched in the gut. A hand went to the strange wreath she wore, pulled at it. Not to remove it, but to make it more snug.

What have I done? thought Julie. I have killed her, and Randy will kill me. A trickle of blood started down Fernanda's forehead.

"Why are you telling me this?" Fernanda said to her.

"Because you need to know the truth," said Julie. "I want him, and will do whatever it takes to have him."

Fernanda turned away. Looked unsteady. The nanny rushed to support her. She turned back and said, "Tell me, Julie. Did you ever have sex with my husband?"

"Many times," Julie said without hesitation. "In India, when you were gone."

The nanny gasped.

"Thank you," said Fernanda. "For being so truthful. Now go."

Julie started to say, I'm sorry, but Fernanda cut her off. The nanny then practically pushed Julie out.

Constance closed the hotel room door and Fernanda stood there, in the middle of that room, absorbing the suffering of not only Christ but of every man, woman and child who had ever loved and had that love betrayed. The Crown was a conduit of some kind, and the words of that hateful woman had opened the gates. How could she withstand such a barrage? All the suffering of all the people who had ever lived, who would ever be, clawed at her heart, eroding the immense love for which she was known.

She stumbled to the bathroom, looked at herself in the mirror. Rivulets of blood ran down her face, from puncture wounds made by the fierce thorns.

"No!" she screamed. "No, no, NO!" She smashed her open hands against the glass, again and again, until the mirror shattered. Even then she did not stop. Until she heard loud knocking at the hotel room door. Had she dared come back, that bitch!

Fernanda stepped from the bathroom, wiped the blood from her eyes, only to see two dark middle eastern-looking men with beards push Constance aside and stand face to face with Fernanda.

"We've come for the Crown."

32 The second miracle

Constance didn't know what was more startling, the appearance of the two bearded men demanding the Crown, or of Fernanda, ferociously facing them, bleeding from her head and her hands. Fernanda looked just like every picture Constance had ever seen of the bleeding Christ: Christ who had been sacrificed, Christ who had been crucified. Constance fell to her knees. "God bless her, God bless Fernanda the Innocent."

The two Turks, brothers, stopped short, taking in the scene of Constance on her knees and of Fernanda, a most striking woman, bleeding just like in the pictures they too had seen of Christ. A spirited, beautiful woman wearing the Crown for which they'd been sent, wearing it as if it were her own.

The older brother said, "Take the Crown." Only to notice his younger brother dropping to his knees.

"A miracle," the younger brother said. "The Crown has claimed her."

"What?"

"Look at her. Her hands! That's where they nailed him. Their Christ."

The baby began to cry, which caught Fernanda's attention. She walked over and took up her little Rocky, held her in her bloody hands.

"See," said the younger brother, "she is the Mother and the Christ."

"You're crazy," said the older brother, closing the hotel room door.

"You take her Crown then."

The older brother took a few steps towards this apparition of a woman, this doppelganger of Christ, but something held him. Her eyes. Her eyes stopped him cold. He felt a sickly uneasiness and had to look away. "You," he said to Constance. "You take the Crown from her and give it to me."

Constance got up and went over, but instead of taking the Crown from Fernanda, she took the baby girl. "I'll feed her," she said.

The older brother watched incredulously as she took a bottle from the diaper bag and began to feed the baby, as if no one else was in the room. He pulled his gun. "Hand me the Crown," he said directly to Fernanda.

"I forgive you," was her reply, blood dripping slowly from her hands, staining the wood floor.

He put his gun away. Set a hand to his forehead. Looked from Fernanda, to Constance and the baby. Shook his head. Pulled out his cell. Made a long distance call. Explained to someone on the other end the situation. Hung up.

"We're to bring her," he said to his younger brother. "Along with the Crown."

"OK," said the brother.

"She won't go," said Constance.

The older brother pulled out his gun again, heavy, shiny, walked over and pointed it at little Rocky's head. "If you come with us, lady, the baby lives," he said. "Refuse and the baby dies. Here, now. Your choice."

Fernanda sighed a heartfelt sigh. The younger brother's eyes teared. Constance held the baby closer to her.

"Well?"

Silence. The seconds dragged. No one moved. Was anyone even breathing?

33 Hateful orders

Taking all this in from the adjoining room, thanks to not one but two bugs and a miniature camera, were the FBI agents assigned to follow Fernanda the Ripper. They watched and reported everything back to their boss. A kind of play by play. They wouldn't have minded too much if the big Turk had pointed the gun at Fernanda, but to threaten a baby, that was going too far.

They asked of their boss permission to intercede.

"He says we should hold," the one FBI man said to the other.

"Damn."

So they sat motionless, listening to the silence after the threat on the baby, waiting for Fernanda to make her choice. Waiting for that or the sound of a gun going off. And then they would have to act. Too late. But then they would act.

But there was no sound. Nor motion. Everyone was frozen in both rooms.

A loud knock on the door made them all jump.

34 The bitch

Julie hadn't walked far down the street when a wave of guilt struck her along with the full ramifications of what she had just done. What right did she have, she, the other woman, to meddle in their marriage? What right did she have to hurt them all?

She stepped into a cafe, took a seat in the corner by the window and ordered an espresso. The waiter brought the tiny steaming cup and set it before her along with the bill. She allowed herself a blissful daydream, remembering the kiss, the taste of Randy still on her lips. Then she washed him away with the bitter espresso. She threw down a handful of Euro coins, and left the cafe.

Where she should have gone right, to the metro, she turned left, back towards the Best Western.

She waved to the hotel clerk. "Forgot something," she said, and hiked up the stairs, not wanting to wait for the elevator. She was crying. She couldn't help herself.

She walked the hall and stopped before the door. Wiped her

tears, but still her eyes were blurry. She knocked on the door, and as soon as it opened she burst in, all bleary-eyed, saying, "I'm sorry Fernanda, so sorry for all that I've done!"

The door slammed behind her.

She rubbed her eyes. Looked around.

What was going on? Who were these men? Was that a gun?

"You, sit here."

Julie sat next to Constance and the baby on the bed.

"Well?" the large man said, pointing the gun at the baby.

"I'll go with you," Fernanda said.

"Not without me, you won't," said Constance. "I am her disciple," she explained to the men. "I go wherever she goes."

"And you?" asked the large man to Julie.

"I'm not. I don't," she said. "I just came back to say I'm sorry."

"Noted," said the man. Then, to Constance, "Give to little Miss Sorry here the baby."

"No," said Fernanda. That's when he struck her.

He yanked then the phone from the wall, used the cord to tie up Julie's feet. He had his brother wash Fernanda's face and hands of their blood. He wrapped a scarf around Fernanda's head, daring not to touch the Crown. He placed coats around both Fernanda and Constance and they went to the door.

"If we are stopped by the police in the next half hour, I will see that you and the baby both die," he said to Julie.

Julie nodded, placed a hand on the baby's soft head.

"Please," a distressed Fernanda tried to say something to Julie, but the door closed before she could finish.

35 Releasing the bloodhounds

CI Mullins waved over a taxi from across the street, one of the many taxis lined up awaiting the end of the veneration at Notre Dame. She and Ed jumped in. "Best Western, Latin Quarter," she told the driver. Turning to Ed, she said, "So you think there are two Holy Crowns?"

"Must be," said Ed. "Only one is real of course."

"What makes you think your serial killer friend has the real one?"

"Fernanda's not a serial killer," said Ed. "Despite what INTERPOL thinks. As far as which Crown is real, would you go to the trouble of stealing all those thorns, even killing for one, to put them on a fake Holy Crown?"

"Nope."

"Somehow Fernanda came into possession of the real thing, completely restored, with thorns and all. And the people behind the thorn thefts, behind the theft of the Crown itself, want it back."

"You think the guy who restored the Crown made an exact duplicate?" asked CI Mullins. "One so identical it could fool the priests of Notre Dame?"

"Who else? Yes, I think he is definitely involved, if not the mastermind," said Ed, finding it hard to sit still in the back of the cab. His fingers danced on his knees, which danced themselves up and down with excitement. "My guess is that someone who knew he would be restoring the Crown contacted him to make a duplicate. A perfect copy to return to Notre Dame, while adding the thorns to the real Crown to sell to the highest bidder."

"But who would buy the Holy Crown?"

"Happens all the time," said Ed. "A world famous painting is stolen from a museum and sold to a rich collector for his own private viewing."

They pulled up to the hotel. A French patrol car was already there. CI Mullins paid the driver, and they rushed inside. Ed flashed his badge at the clerk, who gave Fernanda's room number and pointed upstairs.

A uniformed French policeman stopped them at the door.

"*C'est bonne*," CI Mullins told the man. "INTERPOL." Ed flashed his badge just as his compatriot, one of the FBI Bobbsey Twins assigned to tail Fernanda, came to the door.

"Hi Ed. Didn't know you were still tailing the ripper."

"I'm not," said Ed. "A different case brought me to town. Where's Fernanda?"

"Gone," said the Bobbsey Twin. "Two middle-eastern guys took her and the nanny. Steve is tailing them."

"You idiots let them take her?"

"Boss's orders. He wants to know where they are taking her. Thinks maybe this is all part of the cult she belongs to."

"She doesn't belong to any cult," said Ed.

"Haven't you read the blogs?"

"What's a blog?" said Ed.

"Online posting," said the agent. "PEOPLE magazine and others are posting how Fernanda the Ripper is really the second coming of Christ. That she gives blessings and miracles."

"Ed, what the hell is going on?" asked CI Mullins. "Is your friend a murderer or a saint?"

"I wish I knew," said Ed. They moved on into the hotel room, where a couple sat on the bed fussing with a baby. They both were well dressed – looked like professionals. The man looked up, and Ed cried, "Randy!"

"Ed!"

Randy stood and gave Ed a hug. "I'm so glad you're here. We

need to find Fernanda."

"Yes," said Ed, noticing the blood on the floor. He threw a dirty look at the Bobbsey Twin, then turned his attention to the woman and the baby. "Who's this?"

"This is Julie, an old colleague," Randy said. "The baby is mine. Little Rocky."

"A boy?" asked Ed.

"A girl," said CI Mullins, reaching down to touch the baby's wispy hair.

"Yes a girl," said Julie.

Ed turned to the Bobbsey Twin. "So where are they now?"

"Just boarded a train."

"The metro, you mean?"

"No," said the young FBI agent. "A train."

"Going where?" asked Ed.

"Where?" the agent spoke into his ear-set. "Yeah?" He frowned. "Steve says they bought passage on a fast train and some sleeper trains, all the way to Istanbul."

"To where?"

"Istanbul," said the agent. "Istanbul, Turkey. Their first train leaves in about forty minutes."

CI Mullins looked to Ed, tilted her head, her eyes doing that thing she did, that crinkling that tickled Ed's insides.

"I've always wanted to visit Istanbul," she said.

"I'm coming," said Randy, taking the baby from Julie. "We've got to save Fernanda."

"Me too," said Julie, grabbing the diaper bag.

Ed started to stop them. This was police business after all. But then he remembered Peru. How well they had worked as a team.

"As you wish," said Ed, leading them out the door, down the stairs, onto the sidewalk into a Paris mist. To catch a train. To save a killer or a saint. And, God willing, recover the Crown of Thorns.

36 The ground rules

"Gare de L'Est?" said Ed to his cell. He pulled the phone from his ear just long enough to say to CI Mullins, "Boss says it's the Gare de L'Est train station."

"Gare de L'Est," said CI Mullins to the taxi driver, and the taxi sped off from the hotel, heading North-East through the heart of Paris, with CI Mullins in the front and Randy, Ed and Julie crammed together in the back.

"I told you," said Julie, shifting the baby in her arms. "Gare de L'Est." No one listened to her, instead they focused on Ed as he got the lowdown from his boss.

"So I have permission to tail Fernanda and the Crown?" said Ed, plastering the phone to his ear. "What? I'm not to act on my own?" He made a face, the meaning clear, *I've been at this job far too long, taking orders from idiots.* "No, I hear you," he said. After a few more yes's and no's, he closed his phone.

"A bit of a pickle," he said, leaning forward. "I can assist agent

Steve with the tail, but I can't save Fernanda. Or the Crown. Not right away." He paused to slip his phone back in his pocket. "INTERPOL thinks this could be the big payoff they've invested so much time in. There are two theories actually. Theory one is that Fernanda the Ripper faked the kidnapping. That she is on her way to meet the mastermind behind the Indian cult she belongs to. That the cult plans to use the Crown to pull off something terrible."

"Well that makes no sense," said Randy.

"Agreed," said Ed. "The second theory is that Fernanda is being set up. By Muslim terrorists. That they will use her influence to create a second holocaust. There is much chatter of an upcoming attack, from fanatical Muslims."

"But how?" asked CI Mullins.

"Ever hear of that Jim Jones Christian cult in 78? Jonestown, Guyana. His American followers thought he was the Messiah. He told them the end times had arrived. Talked his faithful into drinking poison Kool-Aid. Mothers poisoned their babies, because they believed he spoke for God. Nine hundred dead."

"But that's just stupid people," said Julie.

"They were good faithful Christians. Misled, but not stupid," said Ed. "Suppose Fernanda obtains a million such blind followers. In the hands of terrorists, she could be more dangerous than a hydrogen bomb."

"You mean they want to use her as a mass weapon of destruction?" said CI Mullins. "Ingenious."

"How about the third theory," said Randy. "That Fernanda is just a woman. And what's this about a crown? Fernanda has no crown."

"Actually she does, Randy," said Julie, touching him lightly on the hand. "I realize now what was on her head when I came to visit. It was a crown of thorns."

"*The* Crown of Thorns," said Ed.

"I'll be damned," said Julie.

"But, but," sputtered Randy to Julie. "What were you doing there, anyway? Why were you visiting Fernanda?"

Julie's face fell. But instead of answering the question, she announced, "The Gare!"

"So what do we do now?" said CI Mullins as the taxi slowed to a stop.

"Get tickets for her train," said Ed. "Then we play it by ear."

"The hell with playing it by ear," said Randy, squeezing from the taxi and stepping out onto the curb. "I'm going to save my wife."

37 Fragile moments

Fernanda sat across from Constance on the train, facing her, with the two bearded kidnappers sitting next to them on the aisle. Her strong feminine hands lay on the Formica-topped table, a spot of red in the center of each white bandaged palm. Her large breasts bled too, but not blood. They bled milk. Baby's milk.

"Once," she said, to no one, to the fine line of dust in the crevice of the edge of the table top, "once as a girl on the border I approached a butterfly. A monarch. I wished to catch it."

She snatched at the empty air.

"Twice I moved too fast, and watched as it fluttered away from me, this way and that, drunken on nectar, stumbling without falling like Father from the bar at night. Or was it zigzagging to avoid my touch, this most beautiful of all creatures, this sweet painted delicacy? The king of the butterflies."

A whistle sounded. Fernanda raised her eyes, sniffed, as if

sensing the presence of someone, then lowered her eyes and continued her tale.

"I slowed my movements, stepped like a prowling cat after the insect. Leaned my body towards the winged king newly perched on an abandoned, footless shoe. On the hard ground. Leaned down towards it with the movement of a sunflower turning to the sun. As I got closer, I reached out with my hand, with my fingers, so slowly that even I could not tell my hand moved. Time passed, my fingers grew nearer the still wings. I became hypnotized by the black-veined pattern on them. The more I stared, the more they took on the look of a jaguar's coat. And I wondered if I was no longer the hunter but the hunted."

A Japanese man in a hat slowed as he made his way down the aisle, stopped a moment to stare at Fernanda, then continued down the aisle.

"The wings were about to flap," she said. "I sensed this before I saw it, so I pinched the wings together, mid-stroke, and raised the creature to my eyes. What a large, proud head, all white spotted. What long antenna, dabbing at the air, trying to take measure of its plight."

She pinched her thumb and forefinger together, held the creature once again before her.

"Where is your crown, *mariposa?* It could only stab its legs in reply. I tossed the dear thing, freeing it."

She gave a flip of her hand. The train jerked ever so slightly.

"I thought it would fly away, but it tumbled to the ground. In my clumsy handling, I had torn a wing. It managed to fly a bit, then crash. Flittered, then fell over. I had captured for a moment the most beautiful thing one could ever hold, and in capturing it, I had destroyed it."

No one spoke. The last passengers came aboard. Their long journey out of Europe would soon begin.

38 Follow that car!

Randy ran towards the entrance to the station, with Ed at his heels. But once inside the open-air expansive hall full of hundreds of people and shops and echoing noise, he didn't have a clue what to do. Just beyond the hall stretched tracks with several trains waiting for departure. An arriving mammoth of a train with a sleek aerodynamic nose screeched to a halt a few feet from a giant rubber stopper. Randy stood there in the hall, head turning this way and that, hoping for a glimpse of Fernanda, hoping to hear her voice.

A heavy hand landed on his shoulder.

"We have to do this together," Ed told him. "That's why I let you come. To help me. I don't believe she is in imminent danger. But a false step by us could make her so."

"OK," said Randy, shaking off his hand.

"Come on, now. We don't have much time to get our tickets."

As they climbed aboard the TGV train bound for Munich, with connections to Istanbul by way of Budapest and Bucharest, CI Mullins realized she was setting off on a three day trip with no change of clothes, no toothbrush, and no gun. At least Ed had his gun. She felt so naked without hers.

They made their way to their seats in the car they'd been told was just behind the one holding Fernanda, Constance and the bad guys. CI Mullins was practically thrown into her seat when the train moved unexpectedly. She settled herself and considered her companions.

Across from her, the mystery woman holding the baby. Julie. She was pretty, in that haughty French way, with a long thin nose, pursed lips and eyes that flashed too much intelligence for her own good. Romantic, probably. Emotionally fragile. Constantly looking over at Fernanda's husband. Love-struck? Dressed conservatively, she gave CI Mullins the impression that she was on her way to the office when all this happened, when she got caught in the undertow of the kidnapping. Would she survive three days without her makeup?

Fernanda's husband, Randy, sat next to Julie; he kept reaching and fussing with the baby she held. His and Fernanda's baby. Good looking guy, early thirties. No tan, so must work a desk job. Appeared smart enough, but not as sharp as Julie.

Then there was her teddy bear, next to her, Ed. A grizzly,

restless guy, who belonged in the wild. He had a good, funny heart, and a strong stubborn streak. An excellent companion. For work or play.

"I'm going to take a quick look," Ed said, rising.

"Me too," said Randy.

"No. She might call out. We can't have that."

Randy relented. CI Mullins watched as Ed walked the aisle to the door leading to the adjoining car.

Ed entered the next car and hunkered down immediately in an empty seat next to agent Steve, giving him a quick nod. The party of interest was not five rows ahead, Fernanda facing him, but with her head down. She wore a scarf on her head under which he could just make out the outline of the Crown. Good. She still had it. Though strange, too. Why hadn't they taken it from her?

He sized up the kidnapper facing him. A burly, bearded man with hard eyes. He wondered why some middle-eastern men had such steely looks. Hard lives? No telling. Ed doubted he could take the man in a fight, so he'd better have his gun handy when the time came to make their move.

Here Ed was, back tailing the bad guys. Always tailing, rarely nabbing.

Fernanda's face rose, her dark beauty, the chilling eyes, paralyzing him. He had never seen such transcendence in any person's gaze. She was definitely special. Not of this world. He finally managed to move, to turn away, to get up and leave the car. Had she seen him? Recognized him? In a way he hoped she had.

39 Munich

Normally Julie liked train travel, but then again, normally she didn't have a crying baby on her lap. At first she enjoyed pretending the child was hers and Randy's. That they were happily married, taking a nice family trip together with their infant daughter. But then the baby cried. Wet? Yes. She changed the baby on the table, with Randy's help. Then the baby cried again. Wet? No. Hungry? Little Rocky clamped down on Julie's proffered knuckle, sucking heartily.

Again Randy helped her, going to the kitchen car in the back to warm the baby's bottle. She liked having Randy next to her, at her beck and call. Wished they could always be together. Maybe Fernanda will be killed, the thought came to her.

No, she mustn't think like that. Dark wishes led to dark places. To regrets and hateful outcomes. She must help Randy save Fernanda. Then, later, if he wants out of the marriage, only then would it be right for them to truly be together. To have their own child, if he wanted.

The baby cried. Wet? No. Still hungry? No. Poo? Yes. Stinky, messy poo.

"Not on the table," said the black woman accompanying Ed. "Go to the bathroom to change her."

When Julie came back she found Randy and Ed in a whispered argument.

"I just don't get it," said Randy. "Why can't we save her?"

"INTERPOL and the FBI want to know where they are taking her," said Ed.

"Her or the Crown?"

"Both," said Ed. "I promise Randy, we'll pounce the second they arrive at their destination."

"In Istanbul?" said Randy. "In three days!?"

"Who knows," said Ed. "They may have bought tickets all the way to Istanbul to throw off any pursuers. Maybe their real destination is somewhere else along the line. Munich or Budapest. Maybe Bucharest."

"And we're to sit and do nothing until they deliver her?" said Randy. "I can't sit and do nothing."

"We're to follow them," said Ed. "That means sitting for now."

Randy got up. To go save his wife.

Ed grabbed his wrist. "Sit down, Randy. I promise I won't let anything happen to her."

They stared at each other; Randy was the first to look away.

"Like Peru?" Randy said, in an accusing way, as he slipped back into his seat.

Ed grimaced, releasing him. "That was different. I was incapacitated."

During the six hours to Munich CI Mullins had plenty of time to plan her shopping trip for the short layover in Munich from where they were to board a sleeper train to Budapest at midnight.

They ended up at a restaurant on a side street, after being assured by agent Steve that Fernanda, Constance and the bad guys were parked in a small restaurant across from the station. After a shared late dinner of bratwursts, giant pretzels and beer, she informed the others of her shopping plans.

"Meet you back at the station," she said, a beer burp escaping before she could cover her mouth. She set out then, by herself, through the town, admiring the quaint shops and architecture.

Disguises were high on her shopping list, since the bad guys had seen Julie at the hotel. She bought floppy hats and sunglasses for them all but especially large-rimmed glasses for Julie. She stopped in a pharmacy and bought makeup for Julie as well. She knew it was important for all of them to be in good spirits, and if makeup would help, why not?

She bought powdered milk for the baby, pampers, and a pacifier. She bought toothpaste and toothbrushes. For her and Ed she bought nuts and chocolate and magazines. She had given the gang orders to buy at least one change of clothes, and small suitcases. She did the same for herself in a department store, just before they closed for the night.

Tired, bogged down with the shopping bags, she found a park bench, in a green space in old town, and rested under a street light. Night pigeons fluttered down before her, out of nowhere, leaving when she offered them nothing. She laughed out loud, once, suddenly realizing where she was and what she was doing and that she must be crazy. On a whim she had opened up to some ol' FBI/INTERPOL agent about her theory on the case of the Thorn robberies, and he had believed just enough. Followed her to Paris, where they spent a wonderful night, last night, at her favorite bar, talking about their pasts, their successes and their foibles. A night that ended with a kiss that he most likely did not remember. When her Thorn theory did not pan out this morning, she had been resigned to return home empty handed. Then next thing she knew, in a whirlwind, they were off on a train across Europe, chasing bad guys, trailing the Crown, heading to the very edge of the continent. To the land of ancient crusades.

She was a crusader, she realized. They all were, inadvertently. Crusaders for the Crown. She laughed again, scaring a passerby, and got up to catch the train.

40 Austria and Hungary, landscape of dreams

The Kalman Imre sleeper train left the Munich Hauptbahnhof just before midnight. In one couchette with four berths, that is, two cushioned planks attached to one wall and two planks attached to the other, lay Fernanda and Constance and their two captors. In the berths of another couchette lay Randy, Julie, Ed and CI Mullins. In a car with regular seats sat FBI agent Steve, nodding off and on. Once in a while Steve got up and walked to the couchette car where our two parties rested. He would haunt the aisle for a while then head back to his lonely seat. They were traveling through high country. He was cold and had no cover.

Constance had never slept on a train before. She had trouble letting go of her fear of falling from the berth. Eventually though the rocking rhythm took her back to Notre Dame, and from there to the realm of the saints.

"I gave her the Crown," said Constance to Saint Eulalia. To Lula.

Lula smiled and swirled around in her white robe, like an exuberant child. "I knew you would. You are a good disciple. Who knows, maybe even a saint one day."

That pronouncement thrilled Constance. Her belief in Fernanda had weakened slightly, when, in the morning, at the hotel, she saw how her Messiah reacted to being told her husband had cheated on her. But then Constance told herself that Fernanda was after all as much woman as she was God. Her reaction was natural for the woman part of her.

"Did you see how the Crown accepted her? How well it fit?" said Constance.

"She is the perfect new owner," said Lula. "She was the perfect sacrifice."

Constance puzzled over that. What sacrifice? Had Fernanda already died? Was this train trip some kind of purgatory? The equivalent of Christ's cave?

"And she will come back from the dead, won't she," said Constance. "In three days. When we reach our destination. She will come back to life as God and end the world."

"If she wants," said Lula. "No one can force her."

"I will force her," said Constance, as Lula faded into the shadows.

The train chugged along. Constance found herself a girl again, on her knees, shooing baby chicks and playing jacks on the hard ground in the back of her grandma's shack. Playing for keeps.

Fernanda tossed and turned on her berth. Occasionally mumbled in her sleep, trying to make sense of what had happened, trying to avoid the same nightmare that followed her all the way from India. She saw people with mutilated bodies reaching for her. Calling to her. Urging her to join them. They welcomed her to their realm of pain and suffering. She awoke, sweating. Removed the Crown, thinking that the bite of its thorns had magnified the dream. But no. As soon as she fell asleep again the ghosts returned, digging their nails into her flesh.

"You are the One. The Chosen One," they said with hollow, cracked voices. Voices of the dead.

"Go away," she told them. "My heart is broken. Look how my love leaks out my breasts."

They clung to her then, fought each other for a place at her breasts, where they sucked with their dead foul mouths, drawing sweet life from her. She screamed.

"Did you hear that?" asked CI Mullins, poking the berth above her.

Ed stirred. "Hear what?"

"A scream."

"I heard it," whispered Julie.

Randy did not stir, nor the baby he had nuzzled against him.

"You should go check," said CI Mullins.

Ed climbed down, awkwardly, still half asleep.

"Take your gun."

He put on his pants and put his gun in his belt, then put his coat on. "I'll be right back," he said, leaving the couchette in his stockinged feet.

He walked the aisle alongside the couchettes. Told himself if it was Fernanda who screamed, if she screamed again, he would have to break into the couchette and save her. Found his way to the one that held Fernanda's party. Listened at the door. A man's accented voice spoke soothingly. "Go back to sleep poor woman," he heard the man say. "These dark times lie heavy on us all."

Not what Ed had expected to hear. He waited a few minutes, outside the door, absolutely still in that quiet place, and felt the night heavy on him as well. He turned around and tiptoed back to his couchette.

"Was nothing," he told them, taking off his pants, climbing back into his berth.

At 9 a.m. the train pulled into Budapest. They were already up and changed into new clothes, with their sunglasses and their hats. They waited to be sure Fernanda's party had left the train, tailed by FBI agent Steve, before they departed themselves. The sleeper train to Bucharest did not leave until 7 p.m. - they had to decide what to do for ten hours in the twin city of Buda and Pest, while making sure the kidnappers did not disappear with Fernanda and her Crown.

41 Budapest, of the dead

"You know you're a dead woman?" the older captor said, leaning so close Fernanda could smell his olive breath. His eyes were bloodshot, tense. His hands moved back and forth like two birds not sure where to land.

The four of them sat on two hard beds in a tiny hotel room that Fernanda and Constance's captors had rented, a place to rest and stay out of sight until time to board the sleeper train to Bucharest.

Fernanda tried to smile.

"The moment you put on that Crown," he said, "you died."

Constance's eyes widened. This matched what she'd learned in her dream last night on the train from Munich, that somehow Fernanda had already been sacrificed.

"Tell you what," he said. "Give me the Crown, now, this minute, and I will give you back your life."

Fernanda reached for the Crown perched on her head.

Constance shouted, "No!" She leaped forward, putting her body between them. "The Crown belongs to Fernanda." She turned to look at Fernanda, nodded for her support.

Fernanda detected the sincerity in those eyes. Her hand went back to her side. "Take the Crown, if you wish," Fernanda told her captor. "I cannot give it to you."

The large man's face showed half a smile beneath his full beard. He shook his head. "Remember, I already tried. I can't take it. Some kind of curse. You must give it, I think."

"You don't really want it," Fernanda told him. "It draws all the suffering in the world into your heart. Saps whatever love you have. Until none is left."

"I would never put on that Crown," he said. "I am not that big a fool. But I need to deliver it to someone who paid a lot of money to obtain it. And to have it put back together."

"The power is in the thorns I bet," said the younger captor.

"What do you know of that, brother?" said the older man.

"I studied Christianity at the University."

"Ah," said the older one. "A Christian scholar."

"No, I'm just hypothesizing. You know that." He went quiet.

"Saint Eulalia gave me the Crown for Fernanda at Notre Dame," said Constance.

"The hell she did," said the older captor. "You stole the Crown in a hat box from the antique shop."

That threw Constance. "No! I tell you an Angel at Notre Dame put it there. He winked at me to let me know."

"I won't argue and it doesn't matter," said the older man. He turned his full focus back on Fernanda. "If you won't give me the Crown before we reach Istanbul, then you will never see your husband again."

"Good," said Fernanda, brushing an imaginary something off her knee.

The older captor frowned. "And your baby? Don't you want to see your baby again?"

She did not answer for the longest time. Finally, she turned to Constance and said, "I can't feel anything, here." She put her hand on her heart, her eyes blinking rapidly, but without tears. She turned feebly to her captor. "You are quite right, sir, when you say that I am dead. Julie's Crowning confession, yesterday morning, quite killed me."

Constance sat down next to Fernanda and wrapped her in her arms, holding her tight. And since Fernanda could not feel enough to cry for the loss of her loved ones, Constance cried for her.

42 Budapest, where two became one

"Attila the Hun was born here," said Phoebe, out of the blue. "Not in Paris."

"I know that, CI," said Ed. "Attila the Hun was an anti-hero of my generation. I read a book about his conquests when I was thirteen. The Christians called him the Scourge of God. His men practically lived on their horses' backs, and attacked with little strategy except wild abandon. I grew up wanting to live my life like that. With wild abandon. Didn't work out that way."

Phoebe had suggested the picnic. Randy opted out, preferring to keep an eye on Fernanda. So they had dropped him at the cafe where agent Steve sat nursing a coffee, watching the hotel across the street where the kidnappers were ensconced. Julie opted out as well, instead taking the baby window shopping.

Ed had told Randy and agent Steve to call the minute the bad guys stirred. In a way he was glad Phoebe had talked him into a picnic. He had spent too many empty days and nights of his life watching and waiting in places like that cafe.

After sandwiches and red wine under a tree, Phoebe and Ed took the funicular to Buda Castle, and old town, on the hill. She thought to check out the famous Thermal Baths of Budapest, but mostly they were just killing time before the train to Bucharest. The funicular reminded Phoebe of the one in Paris that takes you up to Sacre Coeur, the Sacred Heart Basilica.

"He was buried here, too," she said on the funicular, looking down on the bridge and river as they shrank to the size of a painting. A very nice painting. "In a gold coffin inside a silver coffin inside an iron coffin. They buried him. Under the blue Danube."

"Afraid he'd escape?" said Ed.

"No," she said, glancing at Ed. "To honor him and to make sure no one dishonored his bones by digging them up."

"So they threw the coffins in the river, CI?"

"They actually diverted the river, Ed, around the year 450. So they could bury him. Then they let the river return to its bed and killed all who knew the actual spot." She lightly touched his hand on the guardrail of the funicular. "You don't want to call me Phoebe, Ed?"

"I prefer CI," he said, adjusting his sunglasses on his nose. "That way we keep our relationship purely professional."

Phoebe stepped back, the chill in his words hard to take.

"Is that what you want?" She reached and removed the dark glasses, so she could see if he meant what he said. She looked deep into his good eye, but could read it no better than the glass one. Apparently she had made an old fool of herself. She'd have to hide her feelings from now on.

Then his expression changed. A vulnerable droop of his mouth. She read his need. His loneliness. But was he attracted to her, this moment? Not like the other night when he was drunk, but here, now, on a single cup of wine? She took a step closer. He moved closer too, lowered his head.

She met his lips, threw herself into his embrace as if he were a warm spring in this town of springs and she a freezing bather.

43 Bloody good tales

Ed upgraded CI and him to a deluxe compartment with two beds and a private bath for the fifteen hour trip to Bucharest, leaving Randy, Julie and the baby the original four berth couchette he had reserved. However, all four adults and the baby were cramped into the deluxe compartment several hours after departure, sharing a late night snack of baklava and cookies with Theodora bottled water as one by one they made use of the private shower. The train moved slowly, stopping in dark villages only long enough for someone to jump on or off. Agent Steve kept a bleary eye on Fernanda and her captors, to make sure they did not disappear in the night.

"We're passing through Transylvania," said Ed, looking at the etched horizon. "Dracula's home town."

"Vlad the Impaler," said Julie. "That's his real name. A ruler-general in the 1400s. On the side of the Christians. He fought the Muslims that had overwhelmed Constantinople and toppled the Holy Roman Eastern Empire. He got his name from impaling thousands of Muslims. Creating forests of the dying and the dead."

"Dracula was a Christian?" said Randy. "Makes you wonder."

"He was a blood-thirsty son of a bitch," said Ed.

"To Vlad the Christian," said CI, holding up her bottle of Theodora.

"To Vlad," they all toasted and drank their mineral water.

"There is another man from this region who rivals Vlad in his cruelty," said Julie. "Basil the Second, the Bulgar-slayer, Emperor of Constantinople and the Holy Byzantine Empire. When his army captured fifteen thousand Bulgarian soldiers, he had his men poke out the eyes of all but a thousand so they could lead the other men home to their king. Apparently the spectacle of his returning army, helpless, blind, gave the King of Bulgaria a heart attack."

"A good Christian strategy," said Randy.

"To Basil the Christian," toasted CI.

And they drank once again, being silly, drunk not on wine but from train travel in foreign places with companions, from being the good guys on the trail of bad guys. From being in a hopeful love affair in the case of CI and Ed, and a hopeless one for Randy and Julie.

At four in the morning Randy left Julie and the baby sleeping in their berths. He carefully opened and closed the couchette door, crept down the corridor, to the next car, to where he knew Fernanda's couchette lay.

He had to see her. Know that she was OK. He stopped before entering the car, peeked in the window. Noticed a shadow down the way. Another man. Agent Steve probably. So he waited, quietly, ten, fifteen minutes. Was loud, between the cars, the clug-clug-cluging of the train as it moved along the tracks. He felt the rhythmic vibrations of the behemoth train in his feet, like a giant heartbeat. Caught the scent of pine needles in the air from the wild countryside they traversed. Finally the man in the corridor by Fernanda's couchette disappeared.

Randy entered the car, walked slowly, carefully down the dark corridor. Stopped. There was a nightlight on inside Fernanda's couchette, spreading feeble light. He leaned forward to peek in the opening of the curtains. And he saw her, saw his wife, his love, lying on her berth, a scarf around her head, a blanket over her body. As beautiful as ever. How he loved her. Needed her. Suddenly her eyes opened, as if his attention had stirred her. She lifted her head, looked towards the door, looked right at him! Appeared to recognize him. He smiled. Inexplicably, instead of being overjoyed, instead of smiling back, she turned herself over to face the wall.

Randy was crestfallen. Confused.

Maybe she hadn't seen him after all. Hadn't recognized him. Maybe. But something told him she had. And she hadn't cared.

Hadn't felt a thing. Her eyes had been empty, the eyes of the dead.

Not knowing what to do, how to feel about this, he dragged himself back to his couchette, back to his berth. He lay awake the rest of the night, the train lightly jogging his body, telling him he was making progress towards his destination, towards saving his wife and his marriage, but maybe it was already too late.

44 A missed connection, a next flight taken

Constance and the captors stood in the corridor weaving to the rhythm of the train, waiting for Fernanda in the communal bathroom. The train neared Bucharest, where they had only an hour to catch their connection, and the train was running late by fifty minutes.

Constance stepped close to the older captor, and whispered to him, "I think you should know. Fernanda told me last night we're all being watched."

His head turned sideways, distrusting. "You mean, by someone on this train?"

"Yes."

He sized her up, obviously wondering at her intentions. "Why would you tell me this?"

"Fernanda the Innocent must reach Istanbul," Constance said. Gripped his arm for a moment to emphasize the importance. "She must face her fate."

"As must we all," he said, scratching his beard, looking up and down the hallway to see if anyone was watching at that moment. "I appreciate the tipoff, little woman." He spoke in Turkish then with his brother, as Fernanda came out, and Constance took her turn.

"I don't like this," said Ed. The train had barely reached the station in time for their connection with the international sleeper train, the Bospher, and now Fernanda's captors were hanging back, as if they might not take the train to Istanbul after all. Ed and the gang hung back on the train as well, so as not to be seen.

On his phone to agent Steve, Ed asked, "So what are they doing now. Still just sitting?"

The Bospher's all aboard whistle sounded. Any second now the train, their train, would leave without them.

"Ed," said CI. "That train is leaving without us."

Fernanda's captors made their move then, herding Fernanda and Constance out the train, across the quay, and onto the last car of the departing train.

A sprinting agent Steve managed to leap on as well, a quarter of a minute later, with the train building momentum.

Ed and CI, with Julie and Randy, struggled to get off their train quickly with their luggage and the baby, but could only watch as the train to Istanbul pulled far away.

"A sinking feeling, to miss one's train," said CI.

"Damn," said Ed. The train shrank, disappearing around a turn.

"What do we do now?" asked Randy.

"Head for that taxi stand," said Ed.

"We're going to take a taxi all the way to Istanbul?"

"No," said Ed. "We're going to take a taxi to the airport to catch the next flight to Istanbul. Should have done this days ago."

"And miss all the fun?" said CI.

"Can we beat the train?" said Randy.

"By a good twelve hours is my guess," said Ed.

And so they did, arriving at the Istanbul Ataturk airport in the early afternoon, when the train would not arrive until early morning the next day. CI had bought a guide to Istanbul at an airport magazine stand in Romania, and explained to them, in the taxi to old town, several interesting places to visit in the city. They checked into a charming wooden hotel in the historic Sultanahmet region, called agent Steve to make sure all was well on the train, then they ate fresh fish on the roof restaurant that overlooked the strait of Boshorus.

They had an afternoon and evening to kill. Julie chose for Randy and her a shopping trip to the Grand Bazaar, a covered market first opened in 1461, a time when Dracula was still busy impaling his enemies.

Ed chose the Topkapi Palace Museum, a twenty minute walk from their hotel, through what was left of the old Hippodrome. The brochure said that many relics were kept there, including the staff of Moses.

"I'm keen to see the holy Muslim relics," he said.

"More relics?" said CI.

"Can't help it. I've got relics on the brain. From chasing Holy Thorns and Crowns and all."

"Funny what we learn when we travel," said CI, looking over the brochure herself. "I had no idea the staff of Moses was alive and well in Istanbul!"

"And I had no idea that Moses was a Muslim!" said Ed.

"Yeah," said CI. "Seems that Jews, Christians and Muslims share a lot of the old testament and its prophets."

They walked hand in hand, Ed and CI, once Julie and Randy left in a taxi with the baby. Climbed a curved, steep road next to a half-buried, circular wall with those narrow bricks indicative of Roman, or in this case, Eastern Roman Empire or Byzantine architecture. A couple of narrow mummy shaped windows gazed out spookily from thirty feet up.

Besides that wall there wasn't much left of what was once a splendid stadium that could house thirty thousand citizen fans for chariot races and socializing.

In the plaza where once chariots raced, they passed the four thousand year old pink Egyptian obelisk brought to Constantinople in the year 390.

"I love hieroglyphics," said CI. "The stylized animals and cryptic symbols." They paused to appreciate the tall pointed statue with its many carvings.

Ed rested a hand on her shoulder, saying, "In grade school the teachers said I wrote in hieroglyphics."

"I'll bet you did," CI said, placing her dark slender hand on his gnarly white one, while exchanging a look, that special lover's look that only lovers can share.

They got in line to buy their tickets to the Palace whose turreted gateway looked like the entrance to the castle at Disneyland. They entered the gate and walked through different courtyards whose buildings looked like any other old official buildings in the states except for the rounded domes atop them. In the third courtyard they found a long line on the left for the sacred relics.

The interior of the Chamber of the Sacred Relics isn't large but is winding, with the relics in dimly lit modern cases. A holy man can be heard, reading from the Quran, or is it a recording?

People talked, but in whispers.

"Look," said CI. Before them stood the staff of Moses.

"Not as big and imposing as in the movies," said Ed. And it wasn't. Instead it was a highly polished barkless branch, human sized, like a cane for someone with a bad hip. Yes, more of a cane then a staff. Did Moses have a bad hip? Ed didn't know.

Most of the relics were the Prophet Muhammad's. His cloak, two swords, a box, a tooth, and clippings from his beard. From the 600s.

Ed leaned down close to see the clippings. Hair bristles alright, dark black.

"They have nothing of his wives, here," said CI. "They were important in his life. They should have kept something of them as well."

"Here is a carpet of one of his daughter's," said Ed.

"I guess that will have to do," said CI.

"I just had a thought," said Ed.

"Yes?"

"What do Muslims think of Christ?"

"I don't know," confessed CI.

They asked one of the staff on their way out.

"The Quran tells us," said the mild-mannered bearded man, "that Jesus was a prophet of Allah. There is some disagreement though, on whether he died on the cross."

"How about that," said Ed. "Jesus was a Muslim. As well as Moses."

"I was just getting used to the idea that Jesus was born a Jew," said CI.

They left the palace and visited next the pink and gray walled Hagia Sophia, an enormous domed structure with four elegant minarets spiking the corners. A Christian church from 500 to 1400 and then converted to a mosque when the Muslims conquered Constantinople, the building now was a museum. They eavesdropped on a guide who explained that when the church was converted to a mosque, they could have destroyed the mosaics of Christ on the walls but instead chose to simply plaster over them. Later, when restoration of the mosque was undertaken to turn the Hagia Sophia into a museum, the mosaics were uncovered for the first time in five hundred years.

"Wonderful," said CI, looking up at the depiction of Christ over an archway. "Thank goodness it wasn't destroyed."

"Yes," agreed Ed. "A great artist made this, a long time ago."

They left the Hagia Sophia, strolled out onto the plaza, admiring Hagia Sophia's twin, the Blue Mosque, in the distance. A large avenue spread before them, with tracks. They dodged a street car, and walked along the avenue of high priced baklava shops and cafeteria-like restaurants.

One window's display caught their eye, with its large platters of diced chicken and vegetables in sauce topped with fried mashed potatoes, and what looked like juicy stuffed eggplants.

They went inside and pointed out what they wanted, and took a seat. While they ate CI brought up tomorrow's plan.

"So we wait at the train station, and follow them?"

"No," said Ed. "You saw how they acted in Bucharest. They are spooked."

"So?"

"So they won't come all the way to Istanbul, not if they think we're on to them. Most likely they'll get off at the stop before. We'll leave the kids in the hotel and head out early to stake out the stop before Istanbul."

"OK," said CI. "Don't you have INTERPOL reinforcements here? To cover all the bases."

"I believe there may be. But mostly we're relying on agent Steve." He took the last bite of his delicious stuffed eggplant.

"To Steve," CI said, raising her cup of juice.

45 Istanbul and our Human Weapon of Mass Destruction

"I'm sleepy," said Ed, as CI drove the car they'd rented the previous evening to catch the train one stop short of Istanbul. They had received conflicting information about which city this would be, so their plan was to stop in the one farthest out on the line, then race the train to the next one mentioned with less certainty. Not fun, not concrete, but one had to be plastic in a country like Turkey. Bend to the vagaries.

CI glanced over. "Why don't you lay your seat back and catch a few winks. I know how you ol' blokes like to nap."

"Tap, did you say?" said Ed. "Yes, when I was young I was a champion tap dancer."

"Hard of hearing, too, eh?"

"Eh?" said Ed.

She took a hand off the wheel and punched him.

"Hey, why did you do that? I was napping."

Was still pitch black in the countryside, as if they'd been swallowed by a bear. They pulled into town, where the morning mist hung halos on the street lights. From what Ed could see, the town had that British old feel to it more than an American new feel. They found the train station and parked near a single taxi whose driver was asleep at the wheel.

"Schedule?" said Ed.

"They should be arriving in fifteen minutes."

They waited as the half moon over the town seemed to grow in size. Their breath fogged the windshield.

Ed's phone rang, making them both jump.

Was agent Steve. "Yes. I understand. I'm already there. Will do." He closed the phone.

"What did he say?"

"They locked poor Steve in a closet. On the train. He thinks they are getting off. Wants me to tail them in his place. And tell someone to free him."

"We should be able to handle that," CI said.

Ed said nothing. Opened his door as the first vibration of the approaching train reached him. The fresh cold air cleared the windshield. The train whistled its warning. Ed felt a knot in his stomach as the behemoth screeched to a stop before them.

They watched as only four passengers got off. Two men and two women. One of the women wore a head scarf. Fernanda. The four of them headed towards the lone taxi, where the driver stirred, starting his car.

"So we tail them?" asked CI, reaching for the keys to start the car.

"I don't think so," said Ed, moving his jaw side to side, listening to it crack, wondering if anyone's lower jaw ever just fell off. He opened the door a bit wider, put one foot on the pavement. "I think that's enough cat and mouse. You stay here."

Ed reached into his coat and gripped his gun. He was too sleepy, too tired, he told himself, to go tailing after them. The time had come to stand. To put a stop to these shenanigans. To save Fernanda, to save the Crown. Save the poor nanny, too. And, God willing, nab the bad guys. His mind made up, full of stubborn determination, he hadn't taken three steps when all hell broke loose before him.

Five black SUVs came roaring in, out of nowhere, up to the platform, cutting him off.

A dozen men in black swat gear with short barrel automatic weapons poured from the vehicles, surrounding Fernanda and her captors. The older captor drew his gun, but outmanned, he surrendered without a shot.

The Turkey secret service, Ed deduced. That was who this must be. He watched as they talked for a minute with the kidnappers. Watched helpless as they placed Fernanda and the nanny in one of the SUVs and all five vehicles roared away. Even the taxi took off, in the opposite direction. The two bearded men, the original captors, were left standing on the platform in their underwear. The train whistled.

Ed sauntered up to them, his gun ready.

"We need to talk."

46 The heart is a secret prison, a secret prison gets a heart

If only she could stop loving him, Julie told herself. She rested on the bed in the hotel in Istanbul, waiting with Randy and the baby, pondering her future once Fernanda was freed. Her love for Randy imprisoned her, locked her into a life of suffering, as long as Fernanda was around. Was that her fate? A life sentence of longing for Randy?

Baby Rocky began to cry. Julie raised herself, took out a pamper from the bag, to change her. She couldn't believe what hard work it was, caring for a baby. Every hour during the day, and every few hours at night, it wanted something. To be changed, to be fed, to be held. A needy little creature. Maybe we never completely grow out of that, she realized, watching Randy pace the floor. The sun was up and there had been no word from Ed about Fernanda's release.

"She'll be alright," Julie told Randy, the taste of the words bitter on her tongue.

Randy stopped and looked at her. Walked over to her. Sat down.

"And you?" he asked. "Will you be OK? When this is over."

She leaned her head on his shoulder. "And you?" she asked.

Neither had an answer.

When the black SUVs pulled up at the train station Constance thought the American embassy had come to save Fernanda. But the orders the men barked out weren't in English. And once inside one of the vehicles, close up with these men, Constance saw they had dark complexions and slick black hair. Probably Turks. For she knew they were in Turkey, they had passed the border in the train around three in the morning.

The men in the front spoke only on their radio, not a word to Fernanda or Constance. They drove along as the sun came over the horizon and flared at their eyes, washing out their vision.

Fernanda, sitting next to her, buckled in, did not show any emotion. She seemed to have little interest in the happenings of the world. Constance noticed Fernanda's breasts were still leaking, staining her blouse, giving something of an illusion that she had been shot in the heart.

The caravan stopped along the road entering Istanbul. A man came and tied the hands of Constance and Fernanda, and put blindfolds on the both of them.

"Be quiet. Don't try to escape," he told them in an edgy accented voice. The door closed. The caravan continued.

When the vehicles stopped a second time, Fernanda and Constance were escorted down a street and into a building. They descended two flights of stairs, past three or four locked metal doors which creaked when they were opened with keys. Constance heard moaning. And a snigger. And, some person, maybe more than one, was crying. Where were they being taken?

Finally they were shoved against a wall where their hands were untied and their blindfolds removed. Constance realized then that they were in a barren cell, in some kind of jail. The barred door closed, the guards left.

Around them were other cells, full of men mostly. Thin hungry looking men and a few women looking like stick people. Sick people. No furniture, only a bucket in the corner, and the smell, not of something dead, but something infected and dying.

Where were they? What was this place?

A ragged man, with disheveled hair and teeth missing, scooted on his rear across the concrete floor up to the bars separating his cell from theirs, pressed his face against the bars and said, "Welcome to Hell."

His name was Ishmael. Spoke good English. He told them he had been locked in this prison for five years.

"What kind of jail is this?" asked Constance.

"A prison for the criminally inclined," said Ishmael.

"For the criminally insane," said another.

"I'm not insane," protested Ishmael. "Not yet. But I will be if I don't get out of here soon." He coughed, a jagged cough. His eyes watered. He scooted on his rear back to the center of his cell.

Another of the inmates let out a dreadful moan.

"Can't you walk?" asked Constance.

"I could when I came here. But sickness and malnutrition, you know. They break the body. Quicker than old age."

"I'm sorry," Constance told him, feeling a chill and shivering.

Fernanda slid down along the wall, her eyes staring at something Constance could not see. She nodded, removed the scarf, displayed the Crown.

"What is that thing on your head?" asked Ishmael, taking note.

Fernanda did not respond.

"She is Fernanda the Innocent," said Constance. "I am Constance, her first disciple. And that thing on her head is the Holy Crown of Jesus Christ. For she is the Second Coming."

"Oh," said Ishmael. Several of the other prisoners perked up. "Can I hold it?" he asked.

"The Crown cannot be removed," Constance told him.

"Americans, yes?" asked Ishmael, squinting his eyes. "Why were you arrested? Did you kill someone in my country?"

"Fernanda the Innocent is why I am here," Constance said. She went over to the wall and sat down next to her Messiah.

"Ah," said Ishmael, shaking his head. "Psychotics."

"You're all wet," said Constance.

"My breasts," whispered Fernanda. "They're so full they hurt and the milk won't stop coming."

"Milk, did you say?" Ishmael scooted back to the bars. "I thought I smelt something wonderful when they brought you in. Something delicious."

Ignoring him, Constance said to Fernanda, "We need to pump the milk out."

"Here, here," said Ishmael, scurrying to bring an empty, encrusted bowl. Constance was shocked at how skinny his arm was, how bony his hand when he passed the bowl through the bars to her. "Put the milk here."

Constance helped shield Fernanda as she placed the bowl under her right breast. The slightest pressure on the breast forced out the milk, so she milked herself as she'd once seen her father milk a goat. The bowl was full in a matter of minutes. And she still had plenty more, in both her breasts.

"It's full," said Fernanda.

Constance took the bowl and tilted it, with the intention to dump it into the floor drain, when Ishmael cried "No!"

"Give to me, give to me," he said, his face smashed against the bars.

She handed the bowl full of milk to Ishmael. He drank it down all at once, through the bars, spilling half down his face. "Wonderful," he said. "Manna from Heaven."

He handed the bowl back to Constance. Fernanda filled it with the contents of her left breast, and handed the bowl over again. Ishmael took the full bowl and drank it more slowly this time. "Mmmmmm," he said after each sip.

The other prisoners stared, disbelieving. "Milk?" said one. "Please give milk."

"*Sut! Sut!*" pleaded others, "Milk! Milk!"

"Do you have any more?" asked Constance to Fernanda.

"Are you kidding?" she said with a laugh, her first cheerful sign in days. "Give me that bowl." A smile shown on her lips, a sparkle in her eyes. Fernanda was alive again. Their need had brought her back to life.

Constance wrapped her scarf over the top of the next bowl of Fernanda's milk, to keep it from spilling, when she passed it sideways through the bars to Ishmael, who then passed it on to the others. And in this way, in the next hour, bowl after bowl, Fernanda the Innocent fed all the prisoners in that Hell. She fed them all.

Contented then, the prisoners, drowsy like babies after a feeding, one after the other, fell into a deep sleep and dreamed they were in Heaven.

47 Interference

Ed tied the hands of Fernanda's ex-captors, using his own belt and a tattered rag of a sweater he found on the platform. He walked the bad guys over to the car and put them in the back.

"Hello," said CI, turning around in the driver's seat.

They grunted back, both covering their underwear with their tied hands.

"So who was that group that took Fernanda?" Ed asked, sitting back in his shotgun seat.

"MIT," said the older of the two. "Turkey intelligence. This woman with the Crown—"

"Fernanda," said CI.

"This Fernanda isn't what she seems."

"I agree with that," said Ed.

"Why did you kidnap her?" asked CI.

"We did not. Our orders were to obtain the Crown."

"It is the real Crown, you know," said the younger man. "The Crown of the King of the Christians."

"You mean the King of the Jews, don't you?" said CI. "But wait, didn't I hear recently that Jesus is described in the Quran as a prophet of Allah?"

"Yes, of course," said the younger man, "that is why our employer–"

"Shutup!" said the older man.

"We've done no wrong, brother," said the younger man. "Our employer is a rich and powerful patron of the Sacred Trust, the Holy Muslim relics stored in Topkapi Palace."

"We know the place," said Ed. "And the Trust."

"And as such," continued the young man, "our employer took it upon himself to add the Crown of the great prophet Jesus to the Trust collection. He promised much money to a man in Paris to buy and restore it for him."

"You mean he paid a man in Paris to steal and kill for it?" This was CI, again.

"Steal and kill? What are you talking about?" said the older man. "The master restorer told our employer that he could buy the Crown and all the thorns from the Paris diocese. That the church desperately needed money to pay all those lawsuits from the cover-ups. The bad priests scandal, you know?"

"Ah," said Ed. CI and he shared a look. "So the restorer served as a middleman? You were to pay the money to him?"

"The rest of the money, yes. By wire."

"And not to the church?"

"He is to pay the diocese for us. All very secret. No one besides us and the church was to know the restorer made a crown to replace the original that he sold to us."

"And when the restored Crown goes on display in Istanbul?" said Ed.

"The church will say it is a fake. A copy. But we know otherwise."

Ed felt very tired. So much deception. Had the church really sold the Crown? Were the leaders of the church capable of such deception? Of lying to the faithful, pretending they still had the real crown when in fact they had sold it? Well of course they were. The church was run by humans, not by God. But did they do it? That was another question. Or was this all the master restorer's devious play? He cracked his jaw again, and sighed.

"But you don't deny kidnapping Fernanda and the nanny?" he said, hoping the men in the backseat were at least somewhat bad.

"The nanny insisted on coming. And we only took this Fernanda because she stole the Crown from the restorer and she would not give it back," said the younger man. "In a way you can say we arrested her."

Ed laughed.

"You couldn't just take the Crown from her head?" asked CI. "Two big strong men like yourselves?"

"No," said the older man, unblinking. "I tried, and I could not. Something in my heart would not let me."

CI raised her eyebrows, disturbing, momentarily, the play of wrinkles about her eyes.

"The Crown is cursed," said the younger man.

Ed did a double-take. Pondered what he'd just been told. He motioned for CI to step outside with him. "Be right back guys."

They moved a couple of yards from the car.

"Quite the story," said CI. "I think we almost have it sorted."

"We're short Fernanda and the Crown."

"Oh well, yes, there *is* that."

"Appears to me that the master restorer in Paris is also a master criminal," said Ed. "A counterfeiter. Antiques, relics, you name it. Probably has ties to the French mafia. Used those ties to get the Holy

Thorns for the restoration. To make his big sell to this patron of the Sacred Trust in Istanbul."

"Sounds reasonable to me," said CI. "But how did Fernanda come about the Crown in the first place? How does she fit in all this?"

"Still unclear," said Ed. "But I'm not surprised. You'll see, once you get to know her, that Fernanda is special. She draws such things to her."

"Like murder charges? Adulation?"

"And Holy Crowns," said Ed.

"So what are we going to do with these two?" asked CI. "And what about Fernanda and the Crown?"

"You get us to our hotel," said Ed, climbing back into the car, "while I make a call."

The call went to his boss at FBI HQ in the states. He put the phone on speaker for CI to hear as well.

"We've been had," Ed told him. "Turkey secret service grabbed Fernanda as she got off the train."

"Did she have the Crown?"

"Yeah. She was wearing the Crown," Ed said. "Oh, by the way, in case Steve didn't call. He's locked up in a closet on the Bosphor."

"I know," said his boss.

He then repeated to him what the ex-captors had confessed, which was pretty much their innocence.

"I see," said his boss. "I'll tell Paris police to pick up the owner of the antique shop. As far as Fernanda is concerned, I believe INTERPOL talked to the Turkish police. Who probably did an internet search on Fernanda and shit in their pants. Decided she fell into the category of terrorist, anarchist, all of the above. Definitely undesirable. And made her disappear."

"I can't believe—" started Ed.

"You haven't checked the internet in the past couple of days," said his boss. "Too busy with your little European excursion. You should look her up. She's viral. Fernanda is viral. Her sermon, her miracle. Tens of thousands of kids want to be her followers. Worldwide. From all religions. From no religion. All ready to join her church. Her cult. You know how teenagers are. They want to belong to something new. Something uniquely theirs. Rebel against their parents. Fernanda the Ripper, the Innocent, whatever you call her, could become the next Hitler, Ed. Maybe it's best to just leave her buried in a Turkish prison."

"Fernanda?" said Ed. "The leader of a cult?"

"Tell me, with certainty, that she's not," said his boss.

And this, Ed could not do. So he hung up.

48 Not who she seems

The call that morning woke Ahmed in his mansion overlooking the Golden Horn that fed into the Bosphorus.

"Yes," he said, in Turkish, into the old-style handset of the phone he kept by his bed.

"Mulhim of the police is calling, sir."

"OK, pass him to me."

"Good morning Ahmed."

"To you, Mulhim."

"I thought you would want to know we have the woman and the Crown. Locked up. Would you like me to swing by and take you to them?"

"I would like that very much, Mulhim. Bless Allah."

"Bless Allah."

An unexpected call. His men should have arrived today with his

Crown. Why did the police have it instead? Where were his two men? He tried calling them but they did not pick up. "I don't like this," he said out loud, pulling on his pants, getting ready for the arrival of Chief Mulhim.

Ahmed had never been to this particular prison. A most depressing place, he thought, as he walked with Chief Mulhim and an armed guard past locked door after locked door. Finally they reached the pit of the prison, where the criminally insane were kept.

A dim place that Ahmed would have expected to stink, but there was actually a nice aroma, a natural, pleasing smell. Most curious.

"It's too quiet in here," said Mulhim. Ahmed shirked his shoulders, looked around. They stopped in front of a cell with two women who rose to their feet to meet them. One, a dark beauty, wore the Crown, as if it belonged to her. Allah be praised!

"Ishmael," said Mulhim, addressing the disheveled man in the cell next to Fernanda and her companion's. "What's going on? Why so quiet?"

"She is a miracle," said Ishmael, rising to his feet. Standing, he took then a wobbly step forward. "She is Fernanda the Innocent."

"Who?" said Mulhim, shock showing on his face. "You're walking, Ishmael?"

"Thank Allah," said Ishmael. "She cured me."

Ahmed noticed the look of disbelief on chief Mulhim's face.

The guard opened the cell where Fernanda and Constance stood waiting. Ahmed and the chief stepped inside while the guard waited at the cell door. All around them, the other prisoners sat and watched quietly, as if transfixed. As if content.

Ahmed stopped short, the hair on his neck rising as he faced up close this magnificent woman who wore his Crown so fiercely, so proudly. He had never seen anyone so alive. Still she was a thief, who deserved to be judged and punished. And the Crown, well the Crown was his. He would wire the money for it this afternoon, after he placed the Crown into the Sacred Trust collection of Muslim relics at the Palace.

"Good morning," he told Fernanda in English. "It's you who smells so nice, isn't it? Like mountain flowers. Aristolochia I would say. The childbirth species."

"If you say so, sir," she said, exuding contentment herself. Contentment that was jarringly out of place, given where she was.

"You have something of mine," he said, lifting his arm, reaching to take the Crown, when a sharp pain crossed his chest, through his arm, and he gasped. Staggered back. Had she stabbed him? He saw no entry wound and as far as he could tell she had not moved. Only her expression had changed, to one of deep concern.

"Are you OK?" she asked with a strange accent. Neither American nor British.

"Yes. I think so." He raised and lowered his arm. "So what I was told by my man is true. One cannot remove the Crown from you."

"You cannot take the Crown," said Fernanda's young companion, placing a chubby arm around her in a protective way.

"Don't be silly," said Mulhim. He approached Fernanda, and actually managed to touch the Crown before a wave of nausea hit him. He turned, bent over and dry vomited. Coughed. Breathed heavily for a minute. "Guard," he said, huffing, "take that thing off her head."

The guard hesitated.

"Careful," said Ishmael, taking a step forward, steadying himself against the bars. "She is a Holy woman. And that Crown is cursed!"

The guard took a step backwards. "A witch?" he said.

"A kind of witch," said Ishmael.

"So be it," said Ahmed, giving up. "I am a patron of the Sacred Trust and a man of little patience. You keep the Crown, Fernanda the Innocent. For now." Turning to the chief, who had finally recovered, he said, "Let's go."

Once outside Ahmed pulled out his mobile phone and called his secretary. "I want an emergency meeting of the patrons of the Sacred

Trust. Include the Rabbi, the Patriarch. This afternoon."

He listened as she explained he had visitors waiting at his house. Two of his bodyguards were back from Paris, along with friends of someone called Fernanda. Ahmed cursed. His power play to bring the Crown of Christ to the Trust was souring. He decided at that instant to not wire the money. The restorer and the Paris diocese had not delivered on their end of the bargain. He winced at the thought of the pain he had felt when reaching for the Crown. Ahmed would not pay millions for something he could not even touch. The deal was definitely off. But what to do with this Fernanda? This strikingly beautiful thief, and witch, and whatever else she was. And who the hell were her friends?

"Tell them I am on my way."

49 The confrontation

"There's no hiding the fact that you have her," said Ed, shaking Ahmed's hand. A surprisingly strong grip from a rich man. Ed's experience shaking the hands of the rich was that, though they often squeezed hard, the squeeze was a golf club squeeze not a real manly grip. This fellow, Ahmed the rich, had the wide-handed grip of a roughneck.

"I am hiding nothing, and holding no one," said Ahmed, signally for them to sit down again on the luxurious couches in his living-room. So they sat, CI and Ed on one couch, Randy and Julie on another with the baby, while the two body guards, having put on their pants while Ahmed was on his way, remained standing.

"You, your government, same thing," said Ed.

"How little you know my country," said Ahmed.

"I demand, in the name of INTERPOL to whom I am currently assigned, and as agent Ed Pushkin of the American FBI, that she be released immediately," said Ed.

"As do I," said CI. "Chief Inspector Mullins of the London Police Department."

Ed looked at her, frowned a bit.

Ahmed frowned as well. "And you two with the baby?"

"I am Randy, Fernanda's husband."

"*Je suis* Julie. And this is Rocky, Fernanda's baby daughter."

"She has a baby?" said Ahmed. He glared at the older bodyguard. "You took a mother from her baby?"

"I, I," said the man, looking about. "I misunderstood your orders, sir."

"I see," said Ahmed, putting his finger to his lips. Bouncing it there as the full picture came into view. "I think this is all one big misunderstanding." He stood, began to pace slowly before them. "Let me explain my situation. My predicament. Recently, I was offered a priceless relic of great interest to me and others in the Muslim world, for a price I could not pass up. I sent my men to hand carry this priceless item home, only for them to find that your friend, Fernanda, had stolen it. At least, she refused to hand it over when they politely asked. So they call me, explain the situation. And I have to admit I blew my top. In my impatience, I barked at them to bring me the Crown, no matter what it was attached to. I never really meant for them to bring your friend to Istanbul. Certainly not to separate her from her child. I only wanted the Crown." He paused in front of Ed, made a helpless gesture with his hands. "And I certainly didn't mean for my men to bring to my country the dangerous leader of a cult."

"I'm sorry, sir," said the older bodyguard. "For misunderstanding your orders."

"It's just that we couldn't get the Crown from her," said the younger bodyguard. "Something holds you back."

"I know," said Ahmed. "I experienced that this morning, when I visited her at the prison."

"You met her?" said Ed. "So you know where she's being held."

"Yes," said Ahmed. "I just left your friend. An impressive woman. I can't say I've ever met such a woman before. Uses hypnosis, I guess, to make us think we can't take the Crown from her. With those eyes of hers. So imposing. Is she insane, possessed? Perhaps. At the least your friend isn't the simple woman she pretends to be."

"What do you mean?" asked Julie, rocking the baby in her arms. "You said something about a cult?"

Ahmed took a moment to reply. "The chief of police told me that a cult is growing up around her. Worldwide, thanks to the internet. That she is a danger, to governments and religions alike. That is why she has been picked up by the security police and placed in our prison. Not because I sent her."

"But you could take us there. Get her out?" said CI. "Let us escort her home?"

Ahmed tilted his tea, getting the last drop out. Ed watched then how he examined each of them in the room, measuring their worth, financial and spiritual. He was that kind of man.

"I have called a meeting," said Ahmed, "to take place in an hour, a meeting of the patrons of the Sacred Trust. As well as some important non-Muslim religious leaders. To take place here. At my home. A meeting of those with enough influence and power to decide your friend's fate, and the fate of the Crown." He pointed to Ed and CI. "You two can attend, as you are International government representatives. But you two," he said, pointing out Julie and Randy, "you two must go." He told his servant to arrange a cab for the two of them, and told his bodyguards to make sure they left in it.

"More tea?" he asked Ed and CI, "while we wait for the others to arrive?"

50 The interview – part one

While they waited, CI asked Ahmed's secretary for a pad and pen, for notetaking during the meeting of the Sacred Trust. Ed spent time on the phone with both his FBI boss and his INTERPOL manager. Given that neither was helpful in freeing Fernanda, he wondered aloud to CI if one or the other had actually asked the Turkish government to imprison her.

The guests began to arrive. Ahmed escorted them into a large conference room with a white marble table and windows looking out over the Golden Horn.

Two of the three official patrons of the Trust, including Ahmed, wore business suits. The third patron, a high ranking Muslim cleric, an Imam, wore a kind of white kaftan with a round white hat, to go with his silver glasses and wide silver beard. Guest attendee Rabbi Tim of Istanbul wore a black skull cap and a long black wool coat that smelled like a wet beast. The Patriarch of the Constantinople Orthodox Church was a small nearly bald man, wearing black priest garb with a red sash around his waist.

The Christian Patriarch asked a question in Turkish.

"Please let's speak in English for the benefit of our guests from America and the UK," said Ahmed, indicating Ed and CI.

"Why didn't you invite Bishop Joseph?" asked the Patriarch. "His Roman Catholic congregation is tiny but still, you should have, out of courtesy."

"I wanted full Christian representation, but I don't like the man," said Ahmed, taking his seat at the head of the table. "And the subject I am about to broach would be embarrassing to him anyway. So you must represent Christianity in his place."

"I'll do my humble best."

Ahmed rose. "Let's begin. As you all know, I have long desired a relic of the prophet Isa, also known as Jesus, to add to the Sacred Trust. To place with the Muslim holy relics on display at the Topkapi Palace."

"Which I have always thought to be a bad idea," said the patron Imam, sitting at his right, the man with the silver beard and thick glasses.

"Nonetheless," continued Ahmed. "Recently I was offered the chance to buy the Holy Crown."

"Impossible. It is priceless, and a sin to sell," said the Christian Patriarch.

"A priceless relic, in normal times, yes," patron Ahmed went on, "But these are not those times. These are the times of Roman Catholic priests violating children. The times of their leaders covering up these crimes for years. A time of hush money and huge payouts. A time of Roman Catholic dioceses on the brink of bankruptcy, desperate for money. In these not normal times, I was offered the priceless Crown, restored with its holy thorns, for a price I could not turn down."

"A price you should have turned down," said the Imam.

"Perhaps, Imam As," said Ahmed. "But let me finish my tale."

"You've bought the Crown of Crucifixion? But that's a Christian relic, not a Muslim one," said the Patriarch.

"I beg to differ," said Ahmed. "Isa, that is Jesus, was a great prophet of the line of prophets including Abraham and David, a line that led to Muhammed. Jesus was a Muslim as much as he was a Christian."

"Jesus was a Jew," said Rabbi Tim. "You're getting your carriage before the horse."

"He was all three," said Ahmed. "We share prophets, going back thousands of years, we all know that." He motioned to his body guards. "Let them in now."

The door to the study opened, and in stepped Fernanda and Constance, followed by two armed policemen in black swat gear.

Fernanda noticed Ed and gave him a questioning look, to which he could only shake his head.

The moment the Christian Patriarch spotted the Crown he crossed himself. Rabbi Tim whistled. The two patrons sitting to the right and left of Ahmed stood up.

The silver bearded Imam, patron of the Trust, said, "She wears the Crown most elegantly."

"This is Fernanda," said Ahmed. "Just as I bought the Crown, she stole it from underneath me."

"Fernanda the Innocent," piped up Constance. "The rightful heir to the Crown. She is the promised Messiah."

"How dare you say that," said the Christian Patriarch. "That is heresy, daughter."

"Whose Messiah?" asked the silver bearded Imam, the one who did not like the idea of getting the Crown for the Trust in the first place. "You know we are all awaiting our particular Messiah," he said. "We Muslims, the Jews, and the Christians. So it is written."

"She is The Messiah," said Constance. "There can only be one. For all religions. For all the peoples of the world. She brings with her our Day of Judgement."

"A woman Messiah?" said the Imam. "Never."

"Ah," said Rabbi Tim. "It's true we Jews believe that a Messiah is born every generation, in case that generation is the one God deems ready for the Day of Judgement. But I hardly think this woman ..." he paused, taking in this magnificent woman standing before them wearing the Crown of the great prophet Jesus. As if it were her own. "Still, I do see now why you asked me and the Patriarch to come today. In fishing for a Crown, you caught a King."

51 The interview – part two

Fernanda stood unafraid before these powerful, religious men at the table. The presence of Ed puzzled her though. Ed with his gentle machismo, with that human sparkle in his one real eye. She had not a clue how he had come to be here. For that matter, how she had come to be here. And who was the darkly freckled woman sitting close to him, looking a bit puzzled herself, pen in hand?

She realized suddenly she had been asked another question. So many questions. They were wearing her down. Didn't they realize how much energy it took to wear the Crown, how much of her love was being sapped every moment under the torture of it? She turned to the small bald man in the black robe waiting impatiently. Raised her eyebrows to him.

"I said, do you consider yourself the King of the Christians?"

Behind him, out the window, a dark cloud expanded across the city. In the cloud headless bodies and bodiless heads, like in her nightmare. A storm. But not like any storm before.

She heard voices in her head, and felt in her hands the leash of a terrible creature who tugged to be set free. The end, the end, the end, echoed about her.

Constance spoke, answering for her. Poor Constance. She wants so for me to be more than I wish to be.

"Why can no one take the Crown from you?" asked Ahmed, the man who stirred this pot. A proud confident man with a serious look of leadership. Of judgement. Didn't he realize that he was about to be judged? And not by her.

Again Constance spoke, spouting something of little interest to Fernanda. Huge tendrils of lightning licked the air, tasting for the scent of mankind. Fernanda half stumbled, the beast on the leash straining to run amok. How much longer could she hold it back?

"Is it true you can do miracles?"

"I fed some poor men at the prison with my breast milk. For them that was a miracle, I suppose. To have fresh milk in prison."

"Are you against Catholics?"

"No."

"Are you against Jews?"

"No."

"Are you against Muslims?"

"Only when they threaten my baby," she said, feeling her anger mount for a moment. Then she fell quiet and serene.

She could hear them breathing. In the room. Practically hear their hearts beating. Their tiniest movements spoke volumes to her.

"What does she mean?" asked the Imam, "about the baby?"

"Never mind that for now," said Ahmed. "A misunderstanding."

Fernanda closed her eyes. For a moment she was back in Arkansas, in the cabin, with her baby at her breast. She smelled the pines and the long grass. And the baby's milky breath. She missed little Rocky. Missed the innocence in her face, the sound of her cooing. She longed to press her forehead against that of her daughter, to rub her nose on hers. The end, the end, the end.

Ed dared a question, getting her attention. "Tell us, Fernanda. Are you dangerous?"

The wind tore an acorn from the tree in the garden, which struck the window like a bullet, making them all jump.

"Ha," said Ed. They looked outside. Day had turned suddenly to night. Lightning forked, as if for miles, while thunder tried to break the sky.

Fernanda saw that time was running out. Despite that, she felt a wave of contentment. For she realized she could save them. She was the only one who could.

"Yes," Fernanda said loudly, drawing their eyes back to her. "I *am* dangerous. *Peligrosa como no tienen idea.* But only if I claim the Crown."

She stepped forward then, to the edge of the table. Held their eyes as the storm outside went crazy, flinging cars and boats about. "The Crown of Suffering may have chosen me," she said, a tear slipping down her cheek. "But I do not choose the Crown."

She bowed her head, took off the Crown, and smashed it on the hard marble of the table top, scattering Holy Thorns and ancient twigs.

"No!" cried Constance, rushing forward. "You were the one. The Messiah. You were born to bring the End!" She broke down, falling to her knees. Fernanda embraced her.

"It's OK," whispered Fernanda. "It's going to be OK. He forgives me. He forgives us all."

Outside the storm abated.

52 I am INTERPOL

"In the name of international law, I am confiscating what's left of this Crown," said Ed. "And I am escorting Fernanda and her nanny back to Paris."

Ahmed's bodyguards, as well as the Turkish policemen, stepped to intercede.

"No," commanded Ahmed, holding off the men. "He is in the right to take her. I believe she isn't so dangerous now, not without the Crown." He looked at the pieces on the table and laughed. "Glad I never paid for it."

"So that's it?" said the Patriarch. "She spews heresy, destroys the Crown and we are supposed to let her walk?"

"Her companion said those things, remember? She said nothing, that I can think of, that was heretical, about my religion or yours."

"But she destroyed the Crown!"

"Don't worry," said Ed. "I happen to know just the guy to

restore it."

So the meeting of the Sacred Trust adjourned. Ed and CI took Fernanda and Constance, and the pieces of the Crown, away in a taxi. At first inconsolable, Constance cheered up when Fernanda had Ed stop and buy fresh milk for the prison. A quick call to Ahmed and the milk was accepted at the prison door, and distributed per Fernanda's wishes.

53 A happy reunion?

Randy took the call from Ed. Heard the news.

"She's been rescued," said Randy. "They have to drop off some milk, then they'll be here."

Julie tried to smile. She placed the baby on the bed.

"I have to go."

"No you don't."

She felt her body tremble. She had to tell him. He deserved to know. And then she could go. Leave him. Forever.

"Randy, I told Fernanda about us. About India. The morning she was kidnapped."

"Told her what about us?"

"Everything. I think I broke her heart."

She could see Randy's panic at her pronouncement. "How could you?" he said.

She took her coat and opened the hotel room door. "Because I love you," she said. "I always will." The door closed behind her.

The first thing Fernanda did when she arrived was to throw herself on her back on the bed, with the baby, and hold her daughter above her, pressing her forehead against the baby's, then rubbing the baby's nose with hers. To the delight of the both of them. To the delight of all.

Randy shook hands with Ed and CI. "I can't thank you enough."

"And Julie?" asked Ed. CI kicked him in the shin.

"She's gone," said Randy. And to Fernanda, he said, "I know you know. She told me. I'm sorry. Sorry I did it. Sorry you had to hear it from her." He began to cry. "I'm so glad you're safe." He threw himself at her feet.

Fernanda looked at him. Her imperfect Randy. Randy who she once betrayed herself, when she was young. Randy who she loved more than there were sounds in a lifetime, sounds of laughter, sounds of hope.

Cradling their daughter in one arm, she reached and brushed back the hair from his teary eyes. She couldn't say the words then, too soon, but later, later she would tell him what he wished to hear.

54 A honeymoon or two and a moon pie

Ed and CI spent the next few weeks returning the Holy Thorns to their owners, as best they could. The master restorer got a favorable sentence for restoring the broken Crown good as new for the next veneration at Notre Dame in Paris. The French police are still following leads on who in the French mafia actually killed the guard in London, when they stole the Thorn from the British Museum.

In their journey together, CI fell hard for Ed, and he for her. When she chose early retirement, later that year, she moved to the states to live with him. A mistake most likely, she told him, but love does that.

Fernanda did forgive Randy, as hard as that was for her, and a few months later they flew together to Cuzco, Peru, for her natural healer-shaman graduation presided over by her friend, shaman Paro. The trip was a kind of third honeymoon. They left the baby with Chance's wife Crystal, as Constance had gone off to attend Our Lady of the Lake Catholic University in San Antonio, Texas. The internet furor that Constance had helped ignite slowly faded, after the spike created by the story of Fernanda feeding dozens of prisoners in a

Turkish prison with her breast milk. No one comes to Arkansas, to the quartz crystal mine anymore, just to see Fernanda.

Back in Turkey, Ahmed continues to be a patron of the Sacred Trust, and contemplates bidding on a dozen nails advertised on eBay, nails supposedly used to nail Jesus to the Cross. There are also splinters from the actual Cross on sale. But in his heart Ahmed knows that they are not genuine.

This evening little Rocky, for her birthday, ate her first moon pie.

By Ray Else

The First Kiss Mystery Series

Bathing with the Dead

Her Heart in Ruins

All that we touch

Our Only Chance – available in 2017

More to come ...

Short Stories

First Kiss - Galley Beggar Press

Surviving on Mexican Shade – BBC (broadcast)

Also in the works

My Father's Lies

About The Author

Software developer and dreamer of stories. Like most fiction writers, Ray Else's interest in writing began when he discovered books that talked to him, between the lines, books whose authors (spirits, invisible) sparked a conversation that the spirit in him responded to by writing stories himself. For other spirits. A daisy chain conversation.

Ray Else has a B.S. in Computer Science and an M.A. in Technical Instruction / Film History. He speaks English, Spanish and French. An American, he has lived in Mexico and France.

Job-wise he has loaded trucks for UPS, filled rat poison barrels on the night shift, digitized printed circuits, clerked at a department store, was a switcher for Channel 13 on the Texas border, installed inventory systems on oil rigs worldwide, and since 1995 has programmed for the likes of IBM and Rocket Software.

Married, with 4 grown kids and 11 grandkids, he enjoys traveling the world to visit friends and find new stories, occasionally rock-hounding – as shared on his website, rayelse.com.

You may contact Ray Else at rayelsemail@gmail.com.

His author page is: www.amazon.com/author/else

Made in the USA
Charleston, SC
18 January 2016